D1435186

DATE DUE

DEDICATION

I dedicate this book to my caring, supportive husband. Thank you, Sam, for your unfailing love and belief in me and my dreams.

Also, I would like to dedicate this to untold number of genealogists who unselfishly shared our family stories passed down from generation to generation. Especially, I am grateful to those in the Jackson County, North Carolina Genealogy Society for their help in finding my 'roots'.

I dedicate this book to the Hoopers and Watsons in my family line. I have taken our skeletons and legends as themes and created stories to entertain. I changed some first names and dates, but chose to keep our Hooper-Watson family name heritage. Those 'smidgens of truth' are the seeds of great tales.

We have such a colorful family. It would be a waste to not use them.

ACKNOWLEDGMENTS

Writers often live secluded as they write. But standing nearby, available for reassurance, ready for road trips for research, and encouragement with each new page are people that need recognition. Thank you Violet Shults, my sister, for being my research assistant and cheerleader.

To Ginny Barnes, Meagan Rouse, Bruce Wilson, Jeanie Martin, Barbara Orr, Marty and Lori Phillips, and Dr. Lebron Lackey, your inspiration and reassurance kept me going. I could not have continued without your belief in me and my stories. Thank you Emily Phillips for my web site assistance. You're awesome!

To my children, Shaen, Amy, Robin, Marty, and Holly, your companions, and all the grandchildren, this book is for you. I want you to know that dreams are God-given seeds for fulfillment in your lives. May you find a dream and make it become a reality. Search deep in your heart for that passion, and don't let fear of failure cause you to never try.

I would be amiss to not mention my writer groups and leaders. It is important that you understand the great value you are to anyone that writes. Thank you Chattanooga Writers'

Guild, Tennessee Mountain Writers, North Carolina Writers' Network, and the Alabama Writer's Conclave. You have phenomenal writer workshops and group meetings. You create that little glow emanating from new writers as they win an award or honorable mention in your contests. Your incentives prop us up and give us grace and grit to keep trying. I hope every writer has friends and mentors such as each of you

Chapter 1

*Red in the morning, sailors take warning. Red
at night, Sailor's delight.* Mama loved old
sayings and superstitions. She lived her life by
them. The strange thing was, it almost always
happened like she said. This morning the
eastern sky was red, but everything else was
gray. Gray mountains, trees, and fog. I left
here ten years ago this past August and things
were green. And red. Red
blood on the floor, running down Mama's
face, and all over my cousin Tercy's dress.

Letters above the gate read Poverty Hill
Cemetery. I laid my pack and gun by the iron
fence and pushed open the rusty gate.

Wet leaves stuck to my shoes as I weaved
in and out, reading the headstones. I carefully
avoided letting my foot touch a single area that
could possibly be a grave. Mama said it was

bad luck to step across or straddle a grave. She once had told me a story of a little boy that stepped on a grave, and his foot had swollen until it busted.

Unlike the custom in my part of Tennessee of mounding the graves with dirt, here at Poverty Hill they were flat and covered with grass. Tiny green leaves from flower bulbs were pushing upward and would soon blossom.

At the upper end of the cemetery was the Watson section. There were ten graves marked only with field rocks. In time, no one would know who lay there, but I knew. Half were babies born to either my mama or another Watson family. Two were men in their late twenties, one killed by a falling tree in 1855, and the other murdered by an unknown assailant on his way to the mill in the spring of 1857. Another was Uncle Monroe's first wife and baby. She had died in childbirth, and both she and the baby were buried in the same grave. The last two were my Grandma and Grandpa. Their rocks had been picked because of the way they looked like arrowheads and were nearly identical.

Six tomb rocks had been placed after I left, marking the graves of the ones for which I was really looking. Each grave bore a name and chiseled dates. First was my mama, Maggie Watson, born April 5, 1832 - died October 28, 1863. Beside Mama lay Tucker Watson, my papa, and the next two were his brothers, Monroe and Robert. The dates of death of all three men were August 8, 1862. Another grave bore the name T.A. Watson, daughter. She had died two days after both our papas, August 10, 1862. Tercy Arizona, my cousin. The dates of death were deeply carved, even more than the births.

On Tercy's grave was a small bundle of crocus tied with a cotton string. Someone had been here, probably late yesterday as the blooms were not wilted. I stepped backward and squatted down between two graves in the row behind me and stared at the stones. Hate rose like bile into my mouth and burned my nose and eyes. *Senseless deaths.* These were my family. They weren't necessarily Jackson County's most honorable citizens, but neither did they deserve to die the way they had. *Right or wrong, to the last drop of my blood. I am Nathe Milsaps, born a Watson, and I'm ready to serve revenge where none has been dished out.* I swiped at the tears running down my face and rose to stand next to Papa's grave. I couldn't help but wonder where Rachel's corpse lay. No one knew what happened to her.

It was Papa's and his brothers' deaths that had sent me from my home in these North Carolina mountains to live in Tennessee with my cousin, Jemena Milsaps. Her husband, Jonathan, was killed in the war at Cumberland Gap the following year after I moved in. I begged to come back to North Carolina a few

times, but Jemena thought it was not safe.
"There are still some Hooper men wanting
your head, too." She warned me.

I never saw Mama again after I departed
Rich Mountain in 1862. She died the next year
after I left. I was ten years old and had lost
both Mama and Papa.

During the next ten years, I spent
numerous days planning this trip back.
Somebody had to pay for these murders. *What
the law won't do, I, Nathe Watson, will. Some
men deserve to die for the terrible things they
did. It's only right.*

There was a large slate rock lying flat on
the ground behind Papa's headstone. I circled
to look at it. Scratched into the slate rock were
the names of each person that had died at the
hand of the Hooper clan. At the bottom was
written "Remember". Was it put there by
friend or foe? Maybe a warning from one
family to the other? Either could have done it.

I brushed off my woolen breeches. I
walked between Poverty Hill Church and a
row of trees that edged the graveyard. Moss-
covered poplar trees and brushy cedars ran
along the entire edge of the cemetery.
Mountain laurels, as thick as hair on a dog's
back covered the bank all the way to the
branch formed from Buckeye springs about
quarter-mile up from Bearwallow Creek

Across the branch, I heard a cow bawl and
a man's voice hollering, "Come on. Come on."
He banged on a metal milk bucket, and the

cow bellowed again. Familiar sounds of life of early morning in the mountains.

Earlier the wind had been light, almost still. But now the wind had shifted from the west to the North. The temperature was dropping fast. March could do that in these mountains. One day you might be planting your seed potatoes, and the next you could be praying that the freeze didn't get the entire crop.

I switched arms with my pack. It was not heavy by any means. I had returned with no more or no less in kind than what I had carried away. A change of clothes, a coat, my papa's rifle, and a letter. When I left, it was a letter to Jemena. Today it was the last letter from Mama. I pulled the deer hide coat from the pack and put it on. I loaded my gun and placed it on my shoulder. There was a place that I still wanted to visit, and it was a good day's walk, there and back.

I left the cemetery, came back to the forks of the Tuckasegee River, then turned east. At Uncle Monroe's house, there was smoke swirling out the stone chimney, then diving downward, and lying low over the bottom field between the house and the river. Yep. In the winter, when smoke comes up out of the chimney, then falls straight down and settles over the bottom, a measureable snow is soon to come.

As far as I knew, Aunt Corsie, Uncle Monroe's wife, was still alive although she had to be getting up in years. She always was a strong woman. I've seen her hitch a horse and plow from sun-up to sun-down right beside Uncle Monroe. They had eight kids in all, every one of them hell bent to live up to the Watson name for getting into trouble and creating a ruckus.

The next five miles the road sidled along the mountain. Blue lightning streaked the sky, and thunder echoed through the valley at my back. Lighting and falling snow are strange companions.

A strange sense of isolation wrapped itself around me. I remembered the feeling of seclusion that the mountains brought to us and other families in Jackson County. Most of the time, we were in a world all our own. The first recollection I have of the vastness of our nation was when word began to filter in from hunters and traders that came through of trouble brewing among the States. Depending upon who you talked with, you would get a different story, whether they were for the Confederate States or those favoring the Union. Brother against brother. A family divided when the daughter of a Confederate sympathizer married into a family that was of the Union persuasion. Families fought over lead mines and most everything of value to their particular army. These stirrings multiplied the problems my family already had.

The road turned a more northerly

direction at Briarpatch Gap. I stopped to catch my breath. Around me, the snow lay on the boughs of the fir trees and pulled them low toward the ground. Other than quick bursts of wind, it was silent. Still and lonesome.

It sounded liked someone coughed, and something hit the ground behind me. I turned and aimed my gun. I didn't see a soul, but there was a limb on the ground lying on top of the snow about twenty feet away. Yet, there weren't any footprints near about it or any in sight. A chill ran down my spine. I knew the cough had been real.

The snow had slowed to a spit when I reached my home place. The wind stopped blowing, yet I felt a puff of cold air shoot down the collar of my coat. Evil clung to the air much like the smoke that covered the field down by Monroe's place. The hair stood up on the back of my neck. This house had everything to do with the reason I returned. My aim was to make the Hoopers regret they ever touched a hair on the head of a Watson.

I stepped on the boards of the rickety front porch. The door was ajar. I gave it a kick, and it opened. An owl squawked and flew out the window. It didn't look as if anyone had lived here since that bloodbath ten years ago. The furnishings was gone except for an old table turned over with one leg broken. It lay underneath the window where I had escaped. I kicked at a pile of bird droppings and a mass of straw. There was a circle of black on the wood floor. Blood stain. I set my gun in the corner near the fireplace.

I had sat here on the floor near the chairs of my sister Rachel and my cousin Tercy, Uncle Robert's daughter. We had listened to Papa and his two brothers recount a hunting trip the three had taken a week before. It was at the end of the story when we heard footsteps on the porch, the screech of boards, and then heavier, thumping steps of more people. I looked at Mama, and her eyes were fearful and opened wide. Papa stood and reached for his gun that hung over the fireplace but, before he reached it, the door opened so hard it hit the wall with a bang.

Four men rushed in. Levi Hooper used the side of his gun and knocked Papa to the floor. His nephew, Pierce, poked his gun into Uncle Robert's side. Clay, Pierce's dad, pointed a double barrel shotgun at Monroe's temple. Mama grabbed a frying pan and ran toward the fourth man, a cousin to the others, Silas Beck. He sidestepped her and grabbed Mama by the hair and slung her against a wall. A water dipper hit the floor, and Mama's eye hit the nail where it had hung. She screamed with pain and slid down the wall into a heap. Blood ran down her face. Pierce kicked Uncle Robert in the stomach again and again until he buckled his knees to his chest and rolled over with his back to the attacker.

Pierce looked at Rachel and licked his lips. I jumped up and ran full force toward

Pierce. He put out a hand and laid it on my head. I writhed and squirmed, all the time trying to get a hit with my fist somewhere on his body. He laughed and threw me toward the wall.   I fell to the floor beside Mama, gasping for air. A pain like I had never known before went through my right shoulder.

Rachel spat toward Pierce. "You leave me be, Pierce Hooper. I can't stand the sight of you. You touch me and I swear I will stab you."

"Stab me. What with? You don't even got a knife. Besides, you're too dainty to hurt a fly. You are such a pretty little thing. Always did wonder what you'd be like in my arms. You do what I say, and I might decide not kill your Papa."

Papa tried to get up and go to Rachel. Levi slammed his gun against Papa's back and brought him to his knees.

Tercy grabbed the flat iron by the fireplace and threw it at Pierce. He dodged, and the iron hit Silas on the shoulder. Silas leapt at Tercy, knocked her to the floor, and grabbed her by the hair. Pierce commenced to kick her in the stomach until she puked blood all over her dress. Then Pierce grabbed Rachel, dragged her across the floor, and out the front door.

I got up on one knee ready to run out the door and jump on Pierce. Mama grabbed me and pulled me down beside her. "Git yerself to Dicey Coward's house and git us some help."

She grabbed the iron skillet that lay at her side. She took the handle in both hands and began to swing.

I jumped on top of a table by the open window, flung open the shutter, and dove out of it that hot August night. The table crashed behind me. I run like the devil hisself was after me to the side of the house.

"Get the boy, Levi." Clay hollered. But I was gone into the night. Crying, and falling over what felt like every limb and log in Jackson County. Not even a moon for light. There was a path to Dicey Coward's home, and to her house was where I went. Every racing step I felt that any minute one of those Hooper men would grab me by my shirt collar and kill me.

Dicey's house was a good two miles by the trail. I cut down the side of a steep mountain slope to shorten the distance to the house. I felt briars tear at my clothes and face. Blood mixed with my snot and tears.

Dicey was sitting on the porch, and a lantern hung on a nail above her chair. When I got within hollering distance, I commenced to scream. "Ye gotta help us. Help. Help."

She stood and yelled for Hank. "Sounds like that Watson boy, and he's screaming his lungs out." She grabbed the lantern and ran to meet me.

"Nathe, youngun. What are ye doing out this time of the night?" She noticed the blood on my face. "Hank, git out here, I said. The

Watsons are having trouble up at their place. Git your gun and git on up there."

Hank jerked open the front door. His gun was hanging on his shoulder. "What happened at your place, son?' I could only point and grunt as I gasped for breath.

Dicey slammed the door shut. "You don't need to go alone. It's too dangerous. I'll go with you."

"You stay here. I'll take care of this." Hank ran into the dark.

Dicey grabbed my shoulder, and I winced from the pain. "Did they hurt you, boy?"

I shook my head no but pulled my arm against my body to ease the pain.

"Go and get more help. Get around to old man Johnson's place and let him ring the dinner bell."

I took off again, running through the woods to the next house about a mile away.

"Help. Help. Those drunk Hooper men are killing my family." I beat at the door with my left hand and kicked it with my feet until Andy Johnson pulled me inside. One look at my bleeding face and he hightailed it out to a dinner bell and began to ring it. Johnson's house was built against the side of the mountain, and the rest of his land was at the head of the holler, and then ran down toward dozens of small mountain farms below. That bell could be heard for miles, echoing through the valley.

Sary, his wife, ripped off my torn shirt

and wet it. She wiped my face and arms. It stung like the blazes. She touched my shoulder, and I screamed. I looked at the lump on my shoulder. Sary grabbed it, gave one yank, and it popped. My ears roared with a sound like the Tuckasegee during a spring flood, and everything went black.

Ten years ago, but it feels like yesterday. It is carved into my memory with every scratch, cut, and pain I got that day, with every memory of those dead bodies.

The next morning I heard Mama tell Aunt Corsie that they raped Rachel. She said Tercy was kicked a bunch of times in the stomach by two of the Hoopers when she tried again to knock Silas off of Rachel. She died two days later. Mama lost her eye to that nail. All the Watson men were dead by the time Andy Johnson, Hank Coward, and a few other men got to our house. It was all over. People tried to whisper to protect the children, but I had seen that my Papa and his brothers had their heads chopped off. Two of the heads were atop pike poles in our yard. The third head was never found. The heads were so badly beaten that you couldn't tell whose head was whose.

Dicey and Hank Coward washed the bodies for burying and the blood out of the house. Andy Johnson and some other men made three wooden boxes, put the bodies inside, and nailed the boxes shut. I always wondered which head they put in which box and who was buried without.

Hank Coward got a crew of men and dug the graves. All three boxes were placed on the porch at Aunt Linny's, as there was no room in the house. Neighbors came to sit up all night with the bodies until the funeral the following day.

For the funeral, Mama tied a rag of some kind across her hurt eye. She moaned and cried during the service. Blood and tears would run out from under the rag and down her face. Rachel just stared. I sat up straight and wiped my eyes and nose with my shirt sleeve. All I wanted was for this to be over.

After the funeral, we went to Aunt Linny's where the women folk from the church had brought in some food for us. People got plates and went outside and sat in small groups talking quietly and looking at us with pity.

In the house, Mama sat down and pulled me between her legs. She looked me square in the eye. "Those Hooper men will come after you son. You know every one of them by name. They figure I am too scared to say a word, and they're right. But a Watson boy as a witness. They won't take the chance that you might would tell, if the law tries to get to the bottom of this. I'm sending you away. It's the only safe thing to do. And I don't want you to ever come..." Mama threw her apron over her head and cried. She pulled me close to her bosom and whispered into my ear. "Don't ever come back here. Don't tell anyone what you've seen or heard. You must go to Jonathan and Jemena in Tennessee. Take on Jonathan's last name. Jemena hasn't been able to bear children. They'll treat you like a son." She reached into her apron pocket, took out a handkerchief, and blew her nose. She stared at me for a long time, and I stared back. I knew I would never see her again, and she knew the same.

Letters came from Mama to Jemena from time to time. She told us that Tercy died the day after I left, and said that Rachel never was right after that night. She just stared into the air like she was blind. Her fingers picked at her clothes like she was trying to pull strings from the material. She ate food only if Mama fed her. She lost her will to live. But Mama kept her alive as long as she was there with her, making her eat and drink. Rachel would obey but not speak. Mama died the year after I left. The last letter came from Aunt Corsie and said that Mama passed away. She told us that after the funeral Rachel walked away from the graveyard into the woods and was never seen again.

In a world beyond our mountains, a court might have settled the matter, but things were different for us. No justice was ever established, but us Watsons have a long memory.

Chapter 2

Downhill made the body move easier and faster, but even then, the darkness fell before I reached half way down the mountain. Time had gotten away from me while I was at the cabin. I needed to find shelter for the night. Snowflakes flew fast and angry from the north and stuck to my eyelashes and brows. I took the extra shirt from my bag and wrapped it around my half frozen hands. I passed Aunt Corsie's house again, and it was dark with no sign of stirring. It had been a long time since she had laid eyes on me, and a knock on her door at this time of the night might not be safe. Besides, I was not quite ready to come face to face with her. I took a right at the fork, in the opposite direction. I traveled further down the mountain and hoped the snow would ease up.

There were flickers of light between the limbs of the trees. The glow looked to be about a quarter mile away, and all the signs made me think it was flames. A ten minute walk brought me to a fire which burned about halfway between an old house and a pole barn. The run-down house was a one room log structure about fifteen feet wide and twenty feet long. It sat against the mountain with only enough room to walk two abreast between the house and the bluff. A typical mountain home that looked to have been abandoned long enough that it had now fallen into ruin. The front door was gone, as were the windows.

I took a path that overlooked it and noted the roof sagged in the middle with a hole big enough for a body to slip through in the center. I could see the top of a chestnut sapling peeking out through the hole. One end of the house was crushed by a tree that had fallen from the ledge where I stood. Limbs had been cut and thrown to the side of the house. It would take a lot of repair to make such a house livable, even if possible. By the light of the fire, I saw a pile of rotting cornstalks lying by the porch. It had, no doubt, been a corn crib since it had been a house.

Nigh on to about twenty yards to the lower side of the house was the pole barn. It was sturdier than the house and could be useable if someone took a notion to make it a shelter. That is if you could daub it with clay and straw to knock out the wind. If this man lived here, why hadn't he fixed the place up?

Near the barn was a root cellar with the roof tetotally gone. The light from the fire reflected into two tiny eyes that lit up white as they peered out from the cellar steps. Either a coon or some other varmint. Smack dab in the middle of the land between the buildings was the fire. Not just a little cooking fire mind you, but a full blown, blazing one like someone was trying to light the night for miles. That was why I had seen it a quarter mile away. I was pretty sure somebody in my family had once owned this house and land, but I couldn't remember who. In my memory, I could see myself standing in a tater patch behind the barn whilst Mama and Papa talked to Uncle Robert. Nobody lived in the house even then.

If I had any hopes this god forsaken farm might be used to make me a makeshift home, I was mistaken. Beside the fire sat a man that looked near about fifty years old, although it was hard to tell from the side view I had of him. His shirt was green plaid and looked to be made for man a good fifty pounds heavier than him, as did the woolen britches that he had cinched with a rope drawstring that could be seen hanging from his side and laying over the log. He never turned in my direction but spoke with a scratchy voice, like the words were rubbing against sandpaper. "Have a seat boy. Amps' been waiting on you."

"What'd you say?"

He paid no mind to my question. "I expect you are more than likely hungry." He turned to face me and smiled, showing dark uneven teeth with one side tooth on the top missing. "I got some rabbit stew in that thar pot. There be a bucket of water with a dipper over on the porch. A pan of water is over thar too. Wash yer hands."

He didn't have to say it twice. I hadn't eaten since daylight that morning, before I went to the graveyard. I was so hungry that my stomach felt like my throat had been cut. I dropped my pack by the fire but took my gun with me and leaned it against the porch.

The water was as good as I had tasted in many a year. Spring water straight out of the mountains. Water from the Little Pigeon River never tasted this fresh. I took the dipper, poured the icy water over my hands, and went to the fire and held them out to dry.

I sat down on the log and placed the gun by my side. I stuck my feet toward the fire to warm them, and a mist rose from the wet leather. The man handed me a tin cup of stew, and I did not speak until I had eaten three cups full of the hot soup. Steam from the stew and the heat from the fire melted the snow that were frozen to my eyebrows and hair. Water ran down my face like sweat.

He stirred the last of the stew and raked it into my cup. It was so good, like it had been simmering all day long and cooked down to a thick gravy. The man walked to the side of the house and pulled out a dead limb from the pile. One quick whack with the axe he had picked up on his way back made shorter pieces that he threw on the flames.

"What's your name?"

"Just call me Amps. What's yern?"

"They call me Nathe Milsaps."

Amps threw a cup of water into the soup pan and put it back on the fire to boil. The fire light had grown dim, and he moved closer and threw on more wood. He continued to stir the water in the soup pot. In the glow, I looked closer at him. I was taught it was not nice to stare so I took quick side glances. He had dark skin that was cracked like old dried-out, worn leather, tough and stained brown. He had high cheek bones that were hollow beneath. His nose was large like mine, but there was a definite little crook right below where it connected to his forehead, like it had been broken at some time. His eyes sunk into his face making dark circles, framed with bushy gray eyebrows. A too-large woolen hat sat loosely on his head and pushed down on his large ears making them stick out. Greasy, stringy gray hair fell into his shirt collar that looked like scrap threads in the floor next to Mama's spinning wheel. His whole face and body were too thin, pert near sickly. His hands were large. Out of kilter with his thin, bony arms.

Amps left the boiling wash water in the

stew pot and picked up a stick pole and poked at the fire that had gotten bright again. Sparks scattered upward with a snapping sound. "The way this fire is crackling is a sign we can expect another measurable snow tonight. Early March snows can be deep. Watch those blue flames. Yep. A good snow."

That was different than the saying I had heard. Mama told me when a flame turns blue, it meant a haint was nearabouts. But I had decided early on that I did not believe in ghosts. I'd heard more scary stories than you could shake a stick at during cold winter nights in the mountains. Mama loved to feel us scrooch up to her when she scared us with her booger stories. "The snow is already getting deep higher up on the mountain." I said.

"You been up there today? What were you doing on the mountain? Not many people live up there above this level. Do you know someone that lives on Rich Mountain?"

Glad for the darkness, I reached into the bag and pulled out the shirt that I had wrapped around my hands earlier. I spread it out on a log near the edge of the fire to dry. Amps watched everything I did, waiting for my answer. "Just got a little lost. Thought this seemed a well-traveled road and that it might go over the mountain."

"So you are just passing through?"

The flames leaped up, darker blue, and silver white sparks shot upward into the darkness. Instead of answering, I asked, "Have you always lived in these parts?"

He hoiked and spit into the fire. He reached up and scratched his head at my question. "I have been in these mountains for years and years."

The old man raised his chin and looked into my face by the light of the fire. "You look familiar with your big ears and high cheekbones. I don't get out a lot, especially not on this mountain, not for some time. I keep looking for some family resemblance to people I know. It just feels like you are from around here. Real familiar. Are ye?"

Not being sure of who was kin to the Hoopers, and forgetting so many of the people from my childhood, I tried beating around the bush. "I came over the mountain from Tennessee. I think that I might stay in this area a bit. Seems like a pleasant enough place."

"It can be agreeable. But you may find mountain people have quare ways." His dark eyes bore deep into mine. "This place is unworldly and might not be the type of place a young man like you would enjoy. The people that live here spend most of their time a working the ground and trying to squeeze out a living. We don't do much socializing unless there is a need for it. Most everyone knows each other, and we can decipher a stranger when we sees one."

I needed to get my thoughts together on my excuse for coming to the Carolinas before I talked with anyone else. I hadn't expected to see another soul as I came off the mountain. "Sure do thank you for the food. I was hungry, and this hit the spot. I had better move on and find a place to sleep tonight."

The fire looked really good and offered much needed heat. It would have been a good place to bed down, if invited, and if I could escape his watchful eye. Snowflakes were swirling around the edges of the light. It would be possible to build a smaller fire inside the pole barn. It would not be dangerous and could serve as a makeshift place to bed down and would knock off the wind. But to stay could make time for this man to ask more questions. I didn't want to do no talking about myself. This old man was nosy. Still, I would have been obliged for anything that would knock off the falling weather.

"Glad to be of service. There was more food than I needed. Don't mind sharing atall."

"I'd better be pushing off." I picked up my pack and gun.

"Stop by anytime and visit, if you stay around." I looked back after I slipped into the darkness, and he was hunched down and poking at the fire with the stick.

Chapter 3

My head slipped off my pack, and my face fell onto scattered stems of hay. Hay seed and dust filled my nose. "Atchooo."

After I left Amps, I had taken a left at the forks and worked my way around the mountain hoping for a shortcut toward the river and a cave I remembered. But the snow got heavier. It was too dangerous to go further with no stars or moon for light. The only help the snow gave was it made even a little light appear brighter. There was a house and a barn just off the road. I had seen a candle flame that someone had extinguished as I peeped around the side of the barn. The snow had been nigh blizzard strength last night when I climbed up the ladder into the loft for shelter from the snow. Sleep had come easily.

I sat up and stretched, trying to get out the last of the stiffness from sleeping on the hard boards. There were no bales of hay in the loft. It must have been a rough winter if they had already used up the hay stored from last year. It had not yet been warm enough this far up the mountain for any patches of grass to start to grow.

Through a crack on the northwest side of the barn, there looked to be about ten inches of fresh snow on the chicken house roof. *Sure glad I did not have to spend the night out in that weather.* I had been bone tired from walking the day before and slept later than I had meant to. It would have been a sight easier to go away from here unnoticed if I had left before it got light. No rooster had crowed, and there were not any voices from the house to wake me early.

A board was loose, and I pushed it outward to look outside. Clouds were dark and heavy overhead. To the west toward a row of mountains, there was a heavy gray vein of clouds moving across the ridge and toward me. The clouds overhead lay in rows of dark and light, all bubbly and bulging. It appeared they might start snowing even before the storm got here.

A shot of cold air blew in, and I shook like I was in the midst of a fit. Getting up and moving around was the only way to get my body to warm.

I threw my pack to the ground below and held my rifle in my left hand. Planks were nailed to the wall to make a ladder. I turned toward the wall and put my feet from one cross board to the next until I reached the ground. As I reached down to pick up my pack, I heard the click of a rifle being cocked. A cold metal barrel brushed the side of my head. I dropped the bag and put both hands on my gun.

"Don't think about using that gun, mister." I started to turn toward the woman's voice, but she took her rifle barrel and pushed my face back toward the steps. "Whatcha doing in my barn?"

"Don't shoot me, ma'am. I just needed a dry place to sleep. Somewhere out of the cold wind and driving snow. I don't mean you any harm. My gun is not loaded. Besides, I would never hurt a woman."

She uncocked the hammer and pulled the barrel of the gun away from my face. She took the barrel of the gun and shoved it into my shoulder. I turned at the jab and backed up against the wall, still keeping my head down.

"You're not from around here, then?"

I looked at the ground and answered her questions. "No ma'am. I'm from Tennessee."

"What are you doing here? People in these parts don't take kindly to strangers taking up residence in their barn without permission. I could have just shot you, and no one would have been the wiser. Drug your body into the woods for the animals to devour. Not a trace of you would be found."

"I know that's true. But I haven't done nothing. If you just let me leave, I won't be a bothering you no more."

"Look at me. Right here in the eyes." She put the gun under my chin and raised my face. "You don't look like a murderer, but looks can be deceiving."

My eyes continued to look down the cold blue metal of the barrel. Thankfully, her hands were not on the trigger. "I can promise you I ain't never hurt nobody. The gun I'm carrying is only for hunting. I give you my word on it." I looked at her and waited, not sure if I was going to die or not.

"You seem harmless enough. Some say I am too trusting, but don't count on it, mister." She put her gun down and stared into my eyes, like she was trying to make her mind up about my intentions. "I never was one to let another creature suffer if I could help it. My mama taught me better than that. Have you had anything to eat?"

"Not since yesterday night ma'am." I let out a long breath that I had been holding.

"Law, that long? I might as well give you a bite to eat before I send you on your way. Come on to the house." With a feeling of relief, I looked closely at her. She was younger than I expected. And not bad looking for a mountain woman. But the corners of her mouth turned downward in an unhappy, upside down way. Her eyes were tired and dull.

I looked down her body. An apron covered with flowers was tied around her waist and cinched her dress tightly to show a trim waistline. Her hair was brown with tints of red all in it. It was pulled into a bun at the top of her head. Short, damp strands of hair curled around her freckled face. She had on old work boots with the laces untied, and the leather uppers were crackled and splitting. Snow was stuck to the toes.

I stared at her, and she blushed bright red. "Don't make me change my mind, mister. My husband will be right back from the woods. He's gone hunting. But I won't make you wait for him to eat. I am sure you need to be getting along on your way. Come on up to the house."

I followed her to the porch, staying back some so as to not alarm her again. If she got scared, she might not follow through on her offer for a hot meal, and I didn't want to chance that.

"Leave your gun and belongings outside. There's a nail on the post to hang your bag so it won't get wet in the snow. The snow last night blew all over my porch."

"Yes ma'am.

She grabbed a knife that was stuck into the wall with one hand and took meat down that was hanging on the porch with the other. With two quick cuts, she took a block of meat from the side of bacon and carried it and the knife into the house with her.

Inside the house, one fire was going in the fireplace and another in the kitchen stove. It made the tiny cabin warm and inviting. There were two jars of jelly on the table. One looked like blackberry and the other apple butter. She motioned for me to sit. I felt plum homesick. Jemena had put up a hundred and fifty jars of jelly every year. All kinds. Pear preserves. Apple jelly and apple butter. Muscadine jelly. Elderberry and blackberry. Enough for us and to help with some person in need, she said.

She took biscuits from the oven, then pulled an iron skillet from the back of the stove to the front. She sliced thick strips of pork and placed it in the skillet. It sizzled and snapped as it cooked, sending out a smell that would make a dead man hungry. She put two biscuits on a plate and picked up a quart jar of sorghum molasses and placed them in front of me.

"I do like molasses but, if it's just as well with you, I think I would love some of that apple butter."

"Eat what you please from what is on the table. I'll pour you some coffee."

She sat down at the other end of the table and watched me gobble down a biscuit and jelly. Then a biscuit and molasses. A big popping sound of fat frying made her jump up and finish cooking the meat. She placed two pieces of it and two more biscuits on my plate.

I smeared one with apple butter and the other with sorghum.

"It's mighty kind of you to feed me like this."

"Don't know where you are from but, in these mountains, we all share the same lot and usually endure the same hardships, just like we share the same sicknesses and fears. Nothing any one of us has is any fancier than our neighbors. We're all just trying to get by."

Amps had proved that true the night before.

She continued, "Papa always said if any one of us kindle a fire, all who are near about are welcome to come sit by it. As long as there is food in this house, nobody under my roof is going to starve. Not any nearby neighbor or even a stranger. Others around here feel that way too I can tell you. I am proof of that."

"Mama." I looked up in the loft to see two faces staring down at me. The one that spoke was a dark haired, dark eyed little girl that looked to be six or seven years old. Beside her was a young lad of about ten.

"It's alright, Clare. Mama is just feeding a stranger that is passing through. You can come down and git yerself a bite to eat. Come on Davie. You come down, too."

Both children came hurrying down the ladder, and each grabbed a biscuit. Their mama put some blackberry jelly on each one. She stepped out on the back porch and came back with a bowl of butter and a jar of milk. She poured them each a glass full.

The little girl reached and took another biscuit and handed it to me. "Will you put blackberry jelly on this?"

"Lordy, don't be ordering around strangers like that." She looked at me and smiled. "She can be a little bossy sometimes. Here let me fix it."

I handed her the biscuit and watched her spread on the jelly and give it to her daughter. She reached down and lovingly cradled her daughter's blackberry stained face in her hands.

"Mama this is so good. I was so hungry."

The young man wandered over to the door and looked out. "Where's your horse, if you're traveling?" He took a few steps and set himself up between me and his mama. His coal black eyes stared straight into mine without blinking.

"I don't have a horse. I walked over here from Tennessee."

"Why are you coming to these mountains? We don't get many strangers. What's your business here?"

His mother watched our little talk with a smile that she tried to hide with one hand. "I had some wanderlust in me that I needed to get out, I reckon. These mountains are real pretty. Didn't expect this snow though."

He looked back out the window and took a deep breath. "Snow again. What are we going to do?" He sat down at the table across

from me. "We often get these spring snows.
Never did understand why March is spring.
Some years I guess March could bring spring,
but some are like this one. Snowy and cold.
Seems like they should just wait until it warms
up and then say spring is here instead of a day
on the calendar Mama's got."

I wondered how a boy of ten remembered
many springs. Four foot ten at best and his
mama's sandy hair and freckles, but he gave
the appearance of an old man on a little boy's
frame.

"But this snow seems a little deep. It will
sure make our potato planting late this year.
Should have already got them in the ground.
Should have planted in late February or early
March. Even if that book…uh…uh…"

At that, his mother stood up. "The
Almanac…but that will be enough, Davie.
Mister, I guess you better be getting along.
Don't want to hinder you. Be safe in your
travels, and be careful who you trust in these
parts. I told you most of us try to help our
neighbor and do what is right. But there are a
few that don't. Just like any other part of the
world I reckon."

The words sounded like a warning, like
she was thinking of a particular person or
people. "I'll be careful. You don't know
anyone that might be awanting to take on a
hand for the spring planting that will be
starting soon, do you? I may be staying around
awhile, and I will need some work."

She handed me my hat and pulled open the door. "Not off hand. Just ask around down in Speedwell. It's a little more heavily settled, and they might have heard of somebody." She walked out on the porch, picked up the pack that I had hung on the post, and handed it to me.

"Mama, we could use a hand in the fields, couldn't we?" She turned and gave a silencing frown to the boy that had followed us out. "I mean…."

She pushed him back through the open door and leaned her back against it to hinder his view. "Just head down this road, and take to the right at the forks. That will lead you to Speedwell."

"Thanks again ma'am. And my name is Nathan Milsaps, but people just call me Nathe. I appreciate the hospitality. You are better off paid, but what little money I got, I have to be tight with right now. Until I get a place of my own."

"No pay expected."

"Thanks again, Mrs…"

"I'm Addie Fisher. Mrs. Ashe Fisher to be exact."

"Thank you Mrs. Fisher. And tell your husband thank you, too."

"Let's clean the table, children." She spoke hastily, rushed inside, and slammed the door.

Chapter 4

I passed in sight of the old farmhouse and barn where Amps had been the day before. He was already up and standing by the fire with his arms folded and his hands underneath his armpits. Like last night, he wasn't wearing a coat. He was looking up toward the top of Rich Mountain. I didn't say anything to him but headed on down the mountain in the direction of Speedwell.

Uncle Robert's home place was a couple of miles past where Amps was staying. I supposed Aunt Linny still lived there. News had been hard to come by after Mama died. The letters from aunts were few and far between and, when they did come, became harder to read. Jemena said she bet they were getting arthritis and having trouble making their letters where a person could read them.

Smoke was puffing out of the chimney in early morning fashion. No doubt she was knocking off the chill in the house from the freezing temperatures and was cooking breakfast. The house was smaller than I remembered and looked like there had not been anyone to keep up repairs. The front door was wired shut, and the steps were broken. Fields that I remember being cleared were grown over. Only the garden plot appeared still being used for planting

There was banging out by the henhouse, and I walked to the back of the cabin. Aunt Linny had a pick axe in her hand and was breaking ice in a water bucket. She picked up the bucket and placed it near a goat that was tied to a post. Beside her was another bucket which she picked up and took into the hen house. Probably corn or scraps for feed. She stepped inside the chicken house and came out a few minutes later with two eggs in her left hand. She hung the bucket on an iron shoe last and limped toward the cabin..

Ten years had aged her more than I realized it could. Her hair was thin, and her skin looked like worn out saddle leather. Aunt Linny had been a homebody, and Uncle Robert babied her, or so Mama said. She never worked in the fields like Mama or Aunt

Corsie. But it looked like she had spent a lot of time in the sun since Uncle Robert was killed.

I slipped to the edge of the henhouse to get a better look and, just as Aunt Linny got to the back door, she turned and saw me.

"Who are you, and what are you doing on my land?" She laid the eggs on the porch. She reached inside the door and pulled out a rifle. She was quick and pointed the gun at me before I could explain.

"Aunt Linny. It's me. Nathe."

"Nathe? Tuck and Maggie's Nathe?"

"Yes. It's me. How are you, Aunt Linny?"

She kept the gun pointed at me as she came back down the steps and walked up to me. Her eyes looked deep in mine. "It is you. I thought you might have died. Haint heard anything about you or from you since just after your mama died. Come on in boy. Let's catch up a little."

She stood back and let me walk into the house. The common Watson practice, even if only learned through marriage…*Never turn yore back on a single soul you are with. You never know who you can trust. A person that is a friend today may be an enemy tomorrow.* Papa said his dad had taught him that, and it became our family saying.

I went to the fireplace and stuck both hands toward it to warm them. She placed the gun back by the door and came to stand beside me.

"It's not safe here you know. Not even now, after all these years. Hoopers still live around here they say, even though I ain't seen one in years. Think they moved off this mountain. They would consider killing you in a minute, if they knew you were alive. People had it that you ran away after the burying. Some said you died. There are those that thought the Hoopers got you after the funeral, as you were never seen agin after that. Your Mama told me and Corsie where you were, but we never told nary a soul. Not even our children. It was just best everyone thought you were dead. Why would ye come back now?"

I turned my back to the fireplace and felt the warmness coming through my clothes. It might be best if I did not tell her my plans. She might try to discourage me, even though my mind was made up. A true Watson would understand the need for revenge. But she was not a born-Watson.

"I thought it was time to see my kinfolk. You can't run scared all your life. Sometimes you just have to face it. Your house needs some work on it. I could do some of that for you, if you'd let me stay. I could even sleep out in the barn." She paid no mind to what I said.

"Your mama said you didn't go by the Watson name anymore. She said you was a Milsaps. Is that true?"

"It was easier that way, and Mama told me to. Jonathan was good to me. After he went off to war and got himself killed, I couldn't leave Jemena. She needed me. I worked the fields after he was gone and have ever since. She got married again last month, and I thought it was time for me to move on and make my own way."

"You were smart staying there. It was what your mama wanted. Just keep using the Milsaps name, and don't tell anybody who you are. I won't say a word to anyone…just keep it between us two. How long are you planning on sticking around? Not long I hope. Not that I ain't glad to see you, but it's just not safe. It would be best for you to go on back to Tennessee."

"Not sure. I'll know when it's time to move on, and I will. Until then, I will search for some work."

"Work is about as scarce as hen's teeth. Just don't be nosy. People are wary of a stranger coming to these mountains. Word that an outsider is among us gets around pretty quick, and there'll be questions. Every once in a while a family might move in but generally not a single man. You are single, right?"

"Yes Aunt Linny. I'm single. Not had time for courting. It would have hindered my plans, too. Got too much to see and do for that. My time will be better spent now looking for a way to keep food in my stomach."

"You might not ought to be visiting me either. Theys might suspect something."
'Theys were the Hoopers. We both knew who

she was talking about. "It's not likely that I can let you stay here you know. Dangerous to you and to me. You can visit but not often. At best, come only in the cover of darkness and knock three times on the front door, and then come and knock three times on the back door. Understand? I don't let nobody in after dark. Not even my own boys. There's still a lot of goings on in these mountains. People sometimes are just never heard from again. Like your sister. We never found her or her body. Sometimes a person is found dead on a road in the mountains. Word like that travels like the wind."

"People would think I was crazy knocking on that front door. It's wired shut. It needs some fixing."

"Knocking is not for people that are watching the house. It is for me to know it's you."

Does she really think people are watching her house?

She pointed her bony finger at me. "I don't have much company these days and haven't in a long time. I tend to my own business and hardly ever go anywhere. There is nothing I need out there. I dry my own seeds for the garden. I plow my own patch. All summer, I pull grass and tie it up for the mule for the winter. I drink goat's milk. The goats eat weeds and trees. Much more serviceable than a cow. Well you see what I mean. I don't need no outsiders."

I didn't really care to hear about her hermit living. "Is that lead mine still open? I might could get some work there."

Linny grabbed my coat and pulled me around to look at her. "Don't you go asking about that lead mine, do you hear me? You'll be digging your own grave. That mine pretty much petered out before the war was over. They brought in iron gates from Asheville and turned it into a temporary prison. They used it for Union soldiers caught in the mountains until they could move them down to a South Carolina prison. Be careful not to bring up things that could help them find out who you are." She let me go and shoved me toward the door. "Your mama would turn over in her grave if she knew you were here. You git on off this mountain. I have a bad feeling about this visit."

"I'll be careful."

She opened the door and looked around outside the house and into the woods. Then she shoved me out the door. "Nathe, ten years is a long time gone to try to resurrect this quarrel. So don't. I hate them Hoopers as bad as you. They are mean folks. Not a good one in the bunch. They just soon shoot ye as look at ye. There is bad blood between us and them, and there has been for years. Even before your grandpa was born. I don't know why I married into this family. My papa tried to tell me that it would bring me nothing but sorrow. But I wouldn't listen. The foolishness of youth.

You remember now…don't be asking no questions concerning the Hoopers or Watsons." She followed me onto the porch and pushed me to the edge of the steps.

The wind blew icy fog into my face, and my eyes stung. I turned back toward her, away from the ice. A hen ran between us, turned toward me, and crowed. Aunt Linny's eyes widened in fear. She kicked at the hen and shoved me off the steps. "That's a sign boy. 'A crowing hen. Someone is coming to no good end.' Git out of here. I refuse to bury another Watson at the hands of a Hooper. Do you hear? Go away. Go back to Tennessee. If you don't care for yourself, at least don't make me suffer another death. I've outlived my only daughter and my husband. I wish I'd died with them that horrible night. To have to live without them has been worse than death."

It was useless to talk to her. I stopped and peeped back around the side of the house where she stood wringing her hands. She shook her head and mumbled words I couldn't understand. Her hands made crosses in the air. She grabbed an axe off the porch and ran toward the hen that had crowed at me, hemming it in under the edge of the porch and house. With one swift lick to its neck, blood shot into the air. I guess she just wanted to kill the deliverer of what she considered to be a bad sign. Only time would tell. But it did make me feel pretty uneasy about my fate.

Chapter 5

The temperature moderated, and I spent the next few nights camped on the banks of the Tuckasegee River. It was out of the way enough that I didn't often meet people. I needed a plan. If a Hooper took the blood of a Watson, then it was only right that a Watson took the blood of a Hooper. You would think that murder like that of Papa and the other men would cause the law to attempt to find the ones that did the killing. Mama told Jemena the only thing she knew that came of it was that the church sent two elders, Jefferson Henry and Thomas Ballard, to a couple of the Hooper brother's houses with a letter from the church. Jefferson Henry read it to them. "The Hooper family is to be at the next business meeting of the Forks of the River Baptist church next week. The church has been notified of unchristian conduct, and it is requested that you be discharged from the fellowship of the church. There has been an appointed committee to meet with you to answer to these accusations."

They asked as to whom it was that brought the accusations against them. When those men refused to tell them, the Hoopers informed that whoever said they did anything had circulated false reports about them of a slanderous nature, and they wanted those people brought up on charges of slander before the church.

They came to their called meeting and said that they felt justified before God for any and all actions they had committed. They swore they never did no killing though, and that the Watsons, if that were who said they did wrong, just lied. "Twasn't us," they declared. Mama heard that Levi Hooper cursed when he was telling it, and the elders demanded that he repent right there and then. She heard that he cursed again and that his brother Clay had slapped him across the head, at which time he repented. But no one really tried to make any sense of what happened, and it was just forgotten. Mama never heard if any others were called about the matter. Some Hoopers went to the Forks of the River Baptist Church and some to Speedwell Methodist.

The truth might never be known, but what the law of North Carolina nor the church would ever take care of, I would. Feuding is all about memory. The law may have forgotten. The church may have never resolved it and had forgotten. But I figured if you're old enough to remember, you waited until you were old enough to take care of the matter, and then you did it. Not one day had I forgotten.

My first necessity was to find work and a place to live. Nobody knew I was a Watson, so I could move freely and find each and every Hooper. After I found them, I would plan a way to let them know that the Watsons were seeking blood to answer to blood. Death couldn't and wouldn't be sudden. A quick death would be too painless for revenge. Maybe I could scare them and make them feel they needed to always look over their shoulder. Fear gives its own reward to a person seeking vengeance. I had dreamed of shooting enough meat off one of them to feed a hound dog for a week. Not enough to kill quickly, mind you. Just enough to make 'em bleed and suffer for awhile before they died. There needed to be something to remind them of all the terrible things they did. Anything that couldn't be mistaken for someone other than a Watson with a score to settle.

It might be best to get it over with and get away. Stay just long enough to let them know that they were revenged by a Watson and that

it was not just a chance killing. Maybe leave
one alive to tell the tale. Or I could leave a
note on the body or bodies. I was sure glad
Jemena saw to it that I could read and write.
Whatever I decided to do, I would then
hightail it back over the mountain to
Tennessee, or maybe even north to Virginia.

I pulled out my paper and wrote down
ideas. Afterwards, I laid down near the water
to rest. The water sang over the rocks in tune
with my thoughts. "Make 'em pay. Make 'em
pay." The lullaby sang me to sleep. It was the
same tune I had heard over the years in the
crackling fire at night, the crickets that sang,
the wind howling through the cracks in the
house during a storm, and all of nature as they
reminded me that I was the one to even the
score.

xxx

When I woke, the sun was sending light
upward from behind the mountain, with just
enough light in the valley to make out shapes
of trees and rocks. The Tuckasegee was still
singing, but this time its tune had changed to
match the uneasiness in my chest. "Be careful.
Count the cost." I shook my head to clear it.
Watsons were not cowards. I could and would
do my family duty. Papa was counting on me.
I remembered the dreams that I had in
Tennessee the last six months, which drove me
back here. In one, Papa was holding his head

under his arm, and blood shot up in the air and got all over my shirt. His mouth kept saying 'Get 'em boy…You are a Watson ain't ye.' Over and over it talked to me. I would scream and sit up in bed. Jemena would come and make me lay back down. She wouldn't let me tell her the dreams. She thought talking about them would make me dream them again or, like Mama said, telling dreams makes them come true.

Speaking of Jemena, it was time that I did what I promised her the day I left. Today was Sunday morning and I needed to go to church. She made me promise that I would not neglect my duty to God. I didn't tell her how often I would go, but just that I would. And today was as good a day as any. I went to church every Sunday with Jemena and Jonathan. After Jonathan got killed, it was only with Jemena. My prayers for God to take care of the mean Hoopers had gone unanswered. One day, when I was about fourteen, I came to the conclusion that maybe God wanted me to take care of it myself.

Today was the last day of March, and the ground had begun to thaw. It was muddy, but the wind was blowing from the west and should soon dry the damp earth. The water had soaked through nearly everything I owned but my one good shirt and pair of britches. I took them with me to the river to wash up.

I anchored my foot on a root from a sycamore tree and reached down and broke ice near the edge. I pulled up water into my cupped hands. The water was good. I took my wet hands and rubbed it over my face and through my hair. The air was chilly but the sun had topped the trees and felt warm to my back. I leaned against the moss on the north side of the tree until the swirling water stopped, then leaned over and looked down. The water where I had broken the ice was clear and showed my reflection. Jemena had given me Jonathan's straight razor when I was thirteen, even though I had little need for it then. But my face sure needed to get acquainted with it today. Like my hair, my three week beard was ruddy and wiry. No wonder that woman had held a gun on me. That face did look pretty scary.

Downstream about ten feet, a water moccasin slid across the frosty grass and ice at the edge, and slipped into the water. It swam toward the other side with its head held high and its body twisting, as the current carried it downstream.

From my memory of Papa and his brothers, I didn't look like a Watson. Mama's people were the Dooleys, and she said I favored them. This was to my advantage. I could stay longer without someone connecting me to my family. At least I hoped it would be like that.

I left for church. Guilt plagued my mind because of my purpose for going. Worship of

God was far from my thoughts. I wanted to look at the people. To search their faces.

The dampness from the night dried with the light wind and from the sun's warmth. In the bottom land near the river were three deer grazing. They perked up their ears as I passed below them walking by the river. A tree from the other side had been felled by hand and lay across the river making a foot log to cross to the other side. I stopped and caught my breath and watched crows swoop down on freshly plowed ground looking for worms. Behind me, a beaver slid into the water and swam toward the base of the log, easily breaking through the thin ice.

Speedwell Methodist was not far, and I arrived just as service started. Smoke rose over the roof of the church and was pushed down into my face by the fog that lay low over the hill where the church stood.

There was a vacant pew on the left about half way down to the front. I could feel them watching me. I kept my head bent and slid toward the window. The singing was pretty, especially by someone to my right on the pew behind me. I looked back, and it was Addie.

Clare sat on her mother's right. She waved and smiled so big that two little dimples sprouted in her cheeks. Davie's hair was slicked down with grease and combed to the side. He had on a white shirt and clean dark britches, both looking quite a bit too small on his skinny frame. He raised his chin slightly to acknowledge that he saw me. His face was serious as he sat on the other side of his mother from Clare and sang along. Addie chanced a look at me out of the corner of her eye and blushed when she realized I was staring at her. I grinned and turned back around. A quick look across the congregation did not show anyone familiar to me. I had wondered if there would be any Hoopers present. It could be a good way to find them. Next time I would come earlier and sit in the back where I could get full view of them as they left the church.

I waited around after the service, but Addie and the children left without speaking. A few people introduced themselves to me, but none of their names was Hooper.

"Hey mister. I didn't get your name." The pastor stuck out his hand and pumped mine vigorously.

"Nathe. Nathan Milsaps." I answered what I knew his next question would be. Everyone asked. "From Tennessee."

"Well Nathe from Tennessee. We enjoyed having you with us this morning. I am Ollie Marshall, the preacher here. Where are you living?"

"I've been staying down by the river. Outside when the weather is nice, in a cave during falling weather. Trying to look for work."

"Work, huh? Not much of that around here. There is some timber work near

Cashiers, but not sure they are hiring. Let me think." He stroked his chin and wrinkled his brow. "If you can't find work and need a place to sleep and board, you might try Widow Addie Fisher. She might let you bed down in the barn and give you some vittles in exchange for helping her make a garden and a crop. She's an upstanding woman and wouldn't take kindly to any goings on though. I know her and the children are struggling to survive. Her family does not live close by, and she don't have much help."

She's a widow. She had been tight lipped about that fact. Reckon I couldn't fault her for that, me being a strange man.

"You don't have to worry about me. I was raised right. Working for bed and food sounds good to me. I will check with her."

"She lives on Rich Mountain, about half way up. Most people here know where she lives and can point you to the right mountain.

I decided to wait a few days before I broached the subject of work with Miss Addie Fisher.

xxx

I ate jerky brought from Tennessee made by Jemena and occasionally had fish caught from the Tuckasegee that I cooked without seasoning over the fire. It was getting unappetizing to have to eat the same things every day. It was time for fresh meat. Sunday afternoon I cleaned my gun and made a plan to go out the next morning at the break of day. There was not much need for me to kill any large game. A squirrel would be sufficient. My trip to these mountains revealed something I had suspected for some time. I was not a good cook. But I could skin a squirrel in record time and just how hard could it be to boil him in a pot of water. If I swung by the mill and bought a pound of flour, it would make some sumptuous dumplings. There was a little salt in my bag.

The next morning, I awoke to dew dripping from the leaves above and into my face. It felt like spring was making its arrival at last and the morning was without frost. The sun looked wedged behind Rich Mountain with two or three rays shooting straight up into the air. All around it, the mountains had a blue haze as the day's first light was cast. The animals began to stir. Birds were singing and an owl gave its last hoot to the darkness, then flapped its wings above me and flew away to hunt a bed for the day. In the bottom between the river and the road leading up Rich Mountain, a deer rose from its bed from the night and began her forage for food. The warmth had caused new shoots of grass in the bottom land, and a herd of twelve deer across the river were grazing. I settled the butt of my rifle on my toe and made just enough noise to alert the buck of the herd. He raised his head and looked in my direction, moving his head slightly to catch any sound. I tried to not even blink. It was all in vain. The herd ran after him into the woods.

Mornings like this made me realize how much I missed the land of my birth. I hated it when houses were so close you had them in your sight every morning. There were getting to be too many people where I had lived in Tennessee. These mountains were the same as when I left. Very few houses had been built. It was home. As a boy, I ran through these woods, carefree and happy. My closest friend was a light-skinned Indian boy that lived near about three miles from me as the crow flies, down on the river. Inola Hornbuckle. He taught me to use a bow and arrow, and I taught him to whittle. Everything my Papa taught me, I showed Inola. Rough-hewed whistles, sling shots, and animals. It would be good to find him, but asking about anyone by name would arouse suspicions. I needed to lay low until my plans came together and my duty was done. Aunt Linny was right. I felt they would try to kill me if they knew I was in Jackson County again.

The murders never strayed far from my mind. It wasn't about *why* they had killed my family. It was just the fact that they *had*. Surely I was not the only Watson that wanted vengeance for their murders. Should I seek other kin to help? Naw. If they were going to do anything, surely they would have done it by now.

I could ambush the Hoopers, but I wanted more than for them to die. I wanted them to be scared, to plead for their lives like we had, and to suffer. Tit for tat. There was no desire to harm any of their women. I might want retribution, but I would not sink so low as to hurt a woman. I was *not* like them.

Today had started just like most every other day of my life since I went to Tennessee. Remembering. It was how I got through the day being away from Mama, and a way to honor Papa. At least that is how it began. Some time or another it became more than that. It grew to be my life…the reason I got up in the morning and the stories I told to myself as I worked and when I went to sleep. Forgetting would not have been easy, even if I had wanted it to. It was there in front of me when I saw Jemena's face instead of Mama's and Jonathan's instead of Papa's. Or when I looked out the window or door of the house and saw small rolling hills instead of high blue mountains or scattering of trees in the place of giant oaks and poplars.

"Your steps sound like a man toting a heavy burden?"

I near about jumped out of my skin. "What are you doing here Amps? I never heard you come up, and I'm not easily surprised by anyone or anything."

"You were walking like an elephant through the jungle. There is no way you could have heard anything. Have you got the weight of the world on your back, boy?"

"Nope. Just bellyaching to myself about my food supply. Bad prepared fish and dried meat is all I have had for a week or two. Fresh squirrel or rabbit sounds like it would whet my appetite a little better."

"I thought I might do me a little hunting, too." Amps stepped in beside me and walked. "I was thinking you might be long gone by now. Nothing much for a young man like you in these mountains. Most people going west. Why would you make your way east?"

Never will get me no squirrel walking and talking. I preferred hunting by myself. Only coon hunters and children hunted with a partner. I stopped and squatted near an oak tree and decided to get the talking over with and then move on.

The sun had climbed above the mountain and peeked through trees that showed tiny buds of leaves. Amps reached back and pulled his shirttail out of his pants and sat on the ground. He leaned against a fallen tree to my right and stared at me. He had on the same clothes from the first day I had seen him, although they didn't appear to be too awfully dirty. W*here in tarnation is his gun?*

"Have you found a place to bed down besides on that creek bank?"

"I have my options open for some work nearby. If that pans out, I will have a place to stay."

"Is that right? Where would that be?" Amps pulled out a pocketknife and trimmed a twig from a black gum to a short point and picked at his teeth.

"Nothing is settled, and I don't want to be jinxing my opportunity." *Besides it's none of your business.* He was a meddlesome old fool. Amps jerked his head up and looked at me and snurled his lips toward the side of his face and spit.

"I know you think I'm a busybody, but mountain people are quare and, if you don't understand them, you can get in a heap of trouble. Shucks, there are moonshine stills all over this here mountain. Got trappers with their traps all set that would kill you before your next heartbeat and ask questions later. Why don't you just mosey on back to Tennessee where you came from?"

"Why are you so fired up about me leaving? What business is it of yours if I want to stick around?"

"Well, guess it ain't none of my business. But I sure would hate to see you come to a bad end. Your family back in Tennessee would never even know what happened to you."

I wonder if he's a Hooper? Does he recognize me? I searched his face. He didn't seem to be threatening me. That was the first time it had occurred to me that he could be the enemy, and I would never know it until it was too late. I had figured I would right-out know them, and it would be easy to protect myself.

"Amps I never did get your last name. What is it?"

"Just Amps. Haven't used a last name in so long, I figure it don't even matter anymore. Everyone knows me as Amps. I keep mostly to myself. People have probably even forgotten that I abide in these parts."

I stood up. "Over in Tennessee, most places bear a person's last name. If they used where I lived as directions, they'd say 'go by the Milsaps' place and turn right or left'. Don't they do that here?"

"Yeah I guess so. From time to time."

Why was he doing that? He was being contrary and ornery.

I tried a different direction. "What are people's names that live around here? I want to get to know this area and its people. These mountains are as beautiful a place as I have ever seen."

"It is beautiful. But speaking of these mountains, it started out all starry before daylight, but have you noticed it's clouding up now? Clouding up when there's frost and sparkling sun means rough weather before the day is done.

"There weren't no frost where I was." I looked up at layered rows of grey, scudding snow clouds that had gathered.

"Sometimes the weather is different up in the mountain than down lower. But I guess you would not know that, as you are not from around here."

He stepped in front of me. "Sonny, there is a right smart of trouble goes on, so don't be traipsing around and showing up at places that you have no reason to be there. The roads are as crooked as a dog's hind leg, and that make ambushments easy. Feuding has been the way of life for ages here in the mountains, and you could get caught in the crossfire."

Fear stung at my insides. "Feuding, huh? What kind of people feud? Why do they do that? Tell me more." I squatted back down.

He laughed and squatted beside me. "Speaking of nosy."

Actually I had not said he was nosy. I just thought it. He was scary.

"Families fighting and killing other families is almost acceptable and the expected way to settle an argument in these mountains, I reckon. It's mostly ignorance and hot tempered men that have no idea how to reason out the outcome of their angry grudges. Anybody that gets in the way is in danger. Others are drawn into the battle, and the ending always is more bloodshed. They don't consider it needless murder. But it is. Nobody tries to find out what a person meant by what they said or did like a person with a good mind. They consider everything they think to be the golden truth just because they thought it. It ain't always so. Some family clans think they are a law unto themselves. Hoopers and Watsons head up the list." He stared at me and shook his head in agreement to his own words.

I was careful but the question needed to be asked. "Hoopers and Watsons. Who are they? Do you know them?" He was surely not a Hooper if he talked about them like that.

"They'd be feuding families in these mountains."

"Do you know a lot about the Hoopers and Watsons?"

"I know from the time I was knee high to a grasshopper, the Hoopers and Watson's fought over anything and everything. I am not certain how it started, but my Papa said it started over the land grants when both came down after the Revolutionary War. It don't take much to start a feud. A man may feel slighted in some way or thinks someone took advantage of him in a deal. One reason seems as good as the other if you are bent on fighting and killing. After that, bad blood seems to be passed down from one generation to the next.

"The war became the spark at one time. The Watson's owned a mine rich in lead. They were sympathetic to the Confederates and began to mine it to give the South its ammunition. They were mighty upset that the Union army was taking anything and everything to aid their plundering and killing in the South. You see the Hoopers leaned to the Union way of thinking.

"One of the bloodiest fights up to that time came on a day when a Hooper made the mistake of cutting across Watson land as a shortcut to some place he was going. Thinking he was trying to obtain Watson animals that might be useful to the Union army, the Watson man shot him. Too much liquor from a local still and a heart that harbors bitterness can drive a man to do terrible things. Not once did he ask what he was doing on his land. Just made up his mind it was for no good."

"He was drunk?"

"Rumor had it he was. On liquor stolen from a Hooper still."

"Did the law give justice?"

Amps appeared deep in thought, and then laughed. A laugh that didn't seem like he really thought it was funny. "The law don't come into these mountains much. The church deals with some sins and troubles. But. for the most part, it's the hereafter that is left to take care of the guilty. Being killed during a feud, especially if you are as guilty as the one doing the killing, is not a good way to meet your maker I can tell you."

"I take it you don't respect feuding as a way to settle a debt. You don't believe in an eye fer an eye?"

His eyes looked red and fiery, as they bore into mine. "If such a thing as an eye fer an eye was done, the whole world would be blind. Debts are not paid that way, Sonny. It just keeps on going back and forth. That kind of carrying on just ruins families and, in the end, there is just nobody to carry on the family name. It depends on what a man really wants to pay to keep up the feud. How much is it worth to you?"

Amps stood and pulled out his pocket knife again. "I want to give you something. Take this pocketknife. It's not much, but I want you to have it."

"Are you sure? Why would you give a stranger a gift like this?"

"Very sure. I think it will mean something to you someday."

I stood up and took the knife. I walked to the edge of the mountain and looked at the clouds gathering in the west. When I turned around, Amps was nowhere to be seen.

Chapter 6

"Preacher said you might be a needing some help in the fields, getting a crop in the ground and all. So I thought I would stop by and ask you myself."

Addie and the boy was toting water they had fetched from the spring and were almost back to the house. "It seems you must know now that I am a widow. I don't make a habit of lying, but I thought it best that day. You were a stranger and I…well, I'm sorry for telling that story."

"No apology needed. You can never be too careful, being alone and all."

"I probably do need the help but can't afford it."

"I work really cheap. Just let me stay in the barn and feed me, and I'll be much obliged. That would be plenty of pay."

"You would work for just room and board?" Addie bit her lip and looked back at Davie, who sat down his bucket of water. He was shaking his head in agreement. Addie smiled at me. "If the preacher sent you here, he must feel you are honest. I guess you have yourself a place to stay and work to do." She sat down her bucket and wiped her hands on her apron. She reached out her hand and took mine in a strong handshake.

Davie looked down at his water and then at his mama. "I can show him the barn, and help him get his stuff in the loft." Addie picked up both buckets and went toward the house.

I ran after her. "Here let me take that for you."

"Thanks. Wish you had come about an hour ago. You could have helped with the five other trips we've made." She smiled. "Today is wash day." Lines of worry and tiredness melted like a spring thaw when she smiled.

"I wish I had been earlier, too. You shouldn't have to do that kind of heavy work as long as I am here. So Friday is wash day. I'll remember that."

Davie watched me set the bucket on the porch and planted himself in front of me. "It's already time to be tilling the ground for the garden and the corn field. The plow handle is

broke. Do you know how to fix that?" He
waved his hand for me to follow him.

I tipped my hat to Addie and walked
behind the limping Davie to the barn. He
favored his right foot. "Sure I can fix the plow.
What else needs done?" He stopped and let me
open the barn door. I looked down at his foot.
He had stumped his big toe, and it was swollen
and more than likely broke. Two other toenails
were black, and his skin was rough and scaly
from running barefoot in the mountains with
stobs and rocks on every path.

"There's lots to be done. Me and Mama
try really hard to do all the work Papa used to
do and our own chores. I sure am glad we are
getting help this spring. Wish we had another
horse so we could both plow. It would make
the work go faster. Maybe even a mule. Sure
wish you had brought one with you."

I grinned at how he talked fast and didn't
even take a breath. "The preacher said that
your Papa died in the War. I'm sorry about
that. My Pa died in the war too." Jonathan was
as near a Papa as I could have. And the feud
felt like a war, too. Although I could barely
remember what my real Papa looked like,
inside I was a Watson and not a Milsaps, and
always would be. But you have to honor a man
that would take in a boy of ten like his own
and be a papa to him, even if it was only for a
year or two. The troubles in my life had made
me a hand full for even the most patient man
or woman. Looking back I regretted all the

trouble I gave Jonathan and Jemena that first year.

"Your Ma don't need you to help her in the fields, Mr…?"

"Just call me Nathe. Well, she needed me for a number of years. And I helped her until just recently. She married again this past winter. She has a new husband, and he has some boys of his own to help in the fields. I ain't much needed anymore. It's time to make my own way in the world."

"You ain't married, then?"

"No, I'm not married." Young as I was, I probably looked as old as these mountains to him.

Davie looked toward the house. "Mama needs to marry again, or so my Grandma says. But Mama says she ain't interested in any old man in these parts. She says they all think about nothing but feuding and drinking. All but my Papa. He didn't drink a drop. That's why she married him." He looked back at me. "Are you a drinker, Nathe?"

"Nope. Never did like the taste of the stuff."

"That's good. Cause you can't be working on a farm while drinking and carrying on at night."

"I know that to be true. Daylight is coming earlier all the time, and by the end of the day I'll be a-wanting to hit the hay."

Davie grinned. "That's what me and Mama did every day last year during plowing and growing season. She told me she sure was glad that neither me nor Clare needed rocking, because she didn't think she had it in her to do it. She was just too stinking tired.

"In the tack room, there's an old ticking case that I had to throw the feathers away last fall cause it got wet and the feathers knotted up. We ain't had no ducks to get any good soft feathers from. You can fill it with hay, if you'd like to have it to sleep on. Or if there ain't enough hay, there's a pine stand up the road. Pine needles will feel about the same."

He sure could talk a mile a minute. Guess they didn't get much chance for conversation. Davie turned his back to me and drug out the ticking case.

"Son, you need to soak that foot. Wrap it up with clean rags and keep out the dirt, if you ever want it to get well. You got any shoes?"

"Naw. Had an old pair of papa's back in the winter, but they were already mostly worn out when I started wearing them. They were too big, and I got some blisters on my heels at first. But they kept out most of the water and were a sight warmer than no shoes atall. Don't reckon Clare ever had a pair of shoes that I can remember. Mama has a Sunday pair that Grandma gave her, and she has some old boots. She says they are only slightly better than barefoot. They got holes in the soles. She lines them with deer hide or rabbit skin until the lining gets wet, and it gets hard as a rock. Of course she only wears them in the winter."

"Well you soak that foot real good, and then see if your mama has an Irish potato she can scrape and put on a rag and tie to that toe. It will draw that poison and soreness right out. Go on up to the house and talk to your ma about it. I will work out here for the time being."

I picked up the ticking case and shook it, dust blowing like a cloud in the wind. Before bed time, I would take it up the road and find those pine needles. The loft didn't have enough scrap hay to half fill a bed ticking.

The harness was hanging on a peg in the tack room. It was dry and stiff from the dampness. The reins and collar were dried out and worn, and so was the breeching. The hames were in better shape and still solid and could take a lot of load off the horse. There was a can of old bacon grease in the corner. I took a hand full and rubbed it into the dry, cracking leather of the collar, letting the heat of my hands melt the oil so the leather could suck it in. It took the better part of an hour to grease the harness. It felt strong enough to last another season or two if it was kept supple. *The boy probably does not even know to do this. He would have been not much more than a few years old when his daddy died.* I would have to tell Davie to put bacon grease on that toe, too, when he took the potato poultice off.

There was knocking and pecking on the other side of the barn. I peeped through the crack, and there stood a horse pawing on the wall. I moved down and looked through another crack. There was a very small hay stack on the other side of him, stored in the stable. He could smell it. Thank goodness they did have a little fodder left. I threw him two sections of hay and noticed a cut on his front leg. The grease would help this, and I rubbed a fist full over the cut. It didn't seem to be very deep and should heal quickly. He was going to have to work hard the next few weeks. Jonathan used to tell me, "Don't muzzle the ox that treads out the corn." The horse needed plenty of food and proper care if he was going to be strong enough for the field work. There was a patch of green grass down the road. I would send Davie to tie the horse out and let him eat.

"I have some food for dinner if you want to come inside."

I rubbed my hands over the horse's legs and neck, looking for other places that might be sore without looking up at Addie. "I appreciate it, ma'am. I'll be along shortly. I have to finish up with the horse and wash my hands. Then I'll be on up to the house." I raised my head and nodded to her.

She turned to go but changed her mind. "My son is young, and he really needs the help you can give. Him and me has been working this farm for the past two years alone. I appreciate your willingness to work for board. It may well mean the difference in us eating this winter and starving. You are a kind hearted man."

"It works well for us both. We can help one another. If there is anything I am not doing that you feel needs done, just let me know. I am much obliged to you for letting me live here."

She leaned on the side of the barn and watched me check the horse's mouth. "The mare is about eight years old. Papa gave her to me when we came back to the farm. I lived with Mama and Papa after my husband, Ashe, got killed. Davie was small, and Clare was born before Ashe died, but he never got to see her. The mare's name is Maude."

I looked at Addie. She spoke it as a matter of fact and without a lot of emotion.

"I think it's important that you know what happened to my husband, and how we have tried really hard to make a living and a home here."

"I am sorry about your man, ma'am. It must be hard to raise children by yerself."

"The children are good and actually make life a lot easier for me in many ways. They make me want to get up in the morning and face another day. I'm not sure I would have been able to do that, if I had not had them. It's the work and the farm that gets me down. I could have stayed with Papa and Mama, but it just didn't seem right. I'm a grown woman, and I need to make it on my own.

"Ashe and I moved here when we married. Ashe's family was better off than mine. They built this cabin, but papa gave us the land. If we had still owed money on it, I would've lost it, I guess. It's several mountains over from where my family now live, so I don't get to see them much. That is why Papa and Mama didn't want me to move back to Rich Mountain. Mama was worried about me living up here alone with the children."

I got up and stretched my back. It ached from stooping over to check the horse's hooves. It also gave me a chance to look at Addie as she talked.

She smiled. "That's also why papa gave me the horse. It was not so much to use to do farm work, as it was to come home when I failed. And the wagon, they gave it to me when they were shore that I was going to go through with the leaving. You can tell that they didn't think I had it in me to make a way for me and the children. If there was anything that Ashe Fisher and I promised each other when we married, it was to be good providers for our own family. We both knew we wanted a big family and we were going to work hard and make it on our own. We were going to teach our children how to work hard and how to live right and get along with others. Both of us lived lives where our family, especially mine, was not all they should be in many ways. We loved them, but that was not how we wanted our children raised. It was important to us. Now it's important to me."

I nodded that I understood her reason for living alone in the mountains.

"The horse seems in reasonable good shape after the winter. She should be strong enough to pull the plow." I popped the horse on the hips. I walked to the horse's head and rubbed her on the neck.

"That is the second horse Papa gave me. He gave me one when I first married, too. He said to me, 'If Ashe Fisher is ever mean to you, baby girl, you get on old Jake and come home to yore Papa.' But I knew right from the start that would never happen. Ashe rode him when he went off to join the war. I don't know what happened to the horse. I am glad that we have Maude. Couldn't even make a crop or much of a garden without a horse."

"I hope to be able to help. I'll try to show Davie how to work a farm as long as I am working for you, ma'am. It sure is a help to me to have food and a dry place to sleep. I won't go against your principles, if I can help it."

"This was said so you would understand that I won't put up with no carrying on. No liquor drinking or fighting. If you do your work, you won't find the time for such things anyway. But just in case you have any plans to do it, don't. I've worked too hard to lose it all now. Do you plan on staying around here?"

"That depends."

"On what?"

"I don't know exactly. I will know when it's time to move on."

"I see." She bit her lip and folded her arms across her chest.

"Ma'am I won't leave you in a bind. I will stay till harvest."

Her shoulders relaxed. "I thank you for that. Come on up to the house when you are through. Food will be on the table."

"Sure thing, ma'am. Thanks again."

She nodded and went back to the house.

There were several outbuildings that needed repair. There was very little corn left in the crib. Plenty to keep a body busy for the summer.

I took a few shucks and some leather string and tied it up to look like a doll with a walnut wrapped in the shuck for a head. It was a play purty for the little girl. She jumped up and down when she saw it. Her mama nodded and mouthed the words 'thank you.

xxx

That first view of Miss Addie had me believing she was a plain mountain woman, but watching her as we took our meals together gave me a different opinion. She was almost as tall as me and had a beautiful complexion, with just a hint of freckles across her nose and cheeks. Her hair was sandy, but her eyes were dark. The sad look was hardly ever on her face anymore. The weight of trying to feed her children through the previous winter had lifted. We worked together on preparing the ground, getting it ready for the planting season that would soon be upon us. She appeared happier and those smiles changed her whole look. She looked as pretty as a peach. Although I tried to halt my basely instinct, I must admit she also had a nice figure. However brief our time together had been, it had helped her to grow accustomed to my presence, and she was less skittish. She talked about everyday life and joked freely with me and the children. Her nature was pleasant, and she had a kind spirit. My time inside the home showed that she possessed a Bible, which Clare said she read nightly to her and Davie when they were in their beds.

One night after supper, I had already gone to the barn when I heard Clare scream. I looked out the loft to see her mama with a needle, digging a splinter from the side of Clare's foot.

"Clare, be still. If you don't, this needle will end up in your foot just like that ole splinter. Be a big girl, and let me get it out."

She barely whimpered after that. "See there, I got it. Wish I had shoes for you to wear. Maybe then I wouldn't be getting out briers and splinters every day from your little feet. Now get on in the house and up that ladder. I'll come tuck you in."

I came back and sat on the edge of the porch before retiring back to the barn. I watched them through the window. Their beds were at the edge of the loft against a wooden, slatted fence to keep them from rolling off. After reading to them, she tickled each one and tucked them in. That night, I watched as she blew out the lamp and climbed down the ladder. She glanced out the window toward the barn for a moment, and I thought she might have seen me sitting on the porch in the dark. I was ready to give a quick excuse for my presence but found it not necessary, as she turned to her own bed and blew out the light.

Chapter 7

I wish I hadn't given my word to stay till harvest. This meant I had to spread out the time for my plan and make it match up to my leaving after the crops were in. It appeared that I'd be too busy to find the Hoopers. The tools and fields were in bad shape. I worked during the day on the fields and at night on the tools. It would take all summer and into the fall to plant and harvest the crops. Until then, finding time to see where the Hoopers lived and which one would be my target could prove to be a hard job. They surely weren't going to come and find me . Of all the things I could remember, I could not, for the life of me, remember where their houses were.

My conscience pricked me at times when I was thinking about all I planned to do. Not because I was going after revenge, but that Addie would realize I might have been a bad influence on Davie. But I would be long gone after I did it, and the boy would never know it was me. Not even Addie would know. I'd do my best to teach him right things. He didn't have to think about the way of feuding like I'd lived through. I didn't want him fighting either, and he wouldn't learn it from me. I was a hired hand for one summer, and I would keep my secret safely inside my head.

Winter tried its best keep a hold on the mountains. It had a death grip, making for a late spring. It was warm one day and snowing the next. My time was spent catching up odd jobs …things like fixing broken fences. The fence surely hadn't seen any repair since Mr. Fisher had passed. A boy of Davie's age wasn't old enough to carry such responsibility. I took it that the grandpa was too old and sickly to help much anymore. It probably accounts why she was willing to take me on as a boarder and brave the wagging tongues. A single man living with her and her children was shameful. Most of them probably didn't believe our arrangement. But the ones that really knew her would be certain of her respectability. The others were just old busybodies anyway.

She never complained after our first talk at the barn, but it was becoming more understandable that she indeed was struggling to survive, even more than was first apparent. That good breakfast I had the morning after I had slept in her barn was from the goodness of the church. Someone had given her a ham. Another person donated a side of bacon, and some ladies had brought her can food and jellies. Even the milk and butter were given to her. Yet she shared with a stranger.

Breakfast today was a simpler fare. Addie had beat out some corn on a rock the day before and today made mush. There was coffee left from the church gifts. We drank it very weak and light in color to make it stretch.

"Out in the root cellar, there is a bushel of potatoes I can bring in." I said.

"That's my seed potatoes. We can't eat 'em, as much as I would like to some days. Papa taught me that to eat your seed is a death wish. No matter how hungry you get, don't eat the seed you have for the next garden."

"Never had to think about that before. I can see the wisdom in it though. I'm sorry I mentioned it."

"I'm sorry I can't feed you any better than this with you working so hard."

"It'll be ok. It may be necessary to take a day off and see if I can rustle up something from the woods. Kill some fresh meat and dig some roots or something. Do you know what we can find to eat in the woods? My family never had to do that, but I heard of people that did."

"I know some plants. Ashe's mama taught me things like that when we first married. It's what we have lived on for the past year. Not much to have during the winter months with the ground frozen hard as a rock, though. That is why the church helped me like they did. I appreciate that more than words can tell. But now that there is some leafing out of the bushes down lower on the mountain, we can find some things."

"What do you suggest? It is still too rainy to do much in the garden or fields, and it would be a good day for me to find us some food."

"Well, sassafras would be a good start. It's a good spring tonic to get us healthy for the work we will be doing. Only thing is, we won't be able to sweeten it any. I guess we will just hold our nose and drink it."

"My family called it sassy. I know what sassy looks like, so that's no problem. I like it straight without sweetening."

"Too bad me and Davie don't. Clare probably don't remember ever drinking it.

"I saw some poke sallet shooting out of the ground about a week ago. It was along the road near the church. That would be good eating. I can scramble it with an egg or two. Two of the hens are setting, and we can't use their eggs, but the other hen still lets me get three or four eggs a week, at least. I have saved back a couple this week, and I can mix it with the sallet. Even some dandelion would make a good sallet. In the valley, dandelion is growing plentiful."

"That sounds real good."

"I don't like to admit it, but down at the old Watson place, there is an old garden site. It has some shallots that I have gotten before."

I looked at her and wondered how much she knew about the Watson's.

"Don't look at me that way. Nobody else wants them, so I don't consider it stealing."

"I didn't look at you any different way. It's not stealing if they don't need it, I don't reckon. Surely these Watsons don't care that a widder woman uses anything growing there, if they are not going to use it."

"Well, I wouldn't steal anything or do nobody any harm. It's just some shallot onions. I didn't dig them up and take them as my own and leave none there for whoever owns it. I just use what I need and leaves most of the roots to grow more next time me or somebody else needs them."

"That sounds good to me. What else is there?"

"There are ramps up in some of the coves. Like where the church is, only down behind it as it goes toward the river."

"Now ramps is something I never heard tell of. What does it taste like? Not that beggars can be choosers at a time like this."

"We ain't beggars. We are living by our
wits, as Ashe used to say. I have to admit I
was not crazy about ramps when his mama
first fixed them for me. But the taste grows on
you. It's kind of like a wild onion but has a
more garlic taste. It's real good with deer
meat. Or just about any other meat. When
theys are full grown they're about twelve
inches high with leaves like a lily, real wide.
But they have little tiny bulbs. They mostly
grow under maple trees. Don't know why.
Back when I didn't eat them much, I used to
tell Ashe I could smell 'em in his sweat. Made
me feel sick-like. But when I learned to like
them, I didn't feel the same way. I parboil 'em
with the meat. If I have potatoes, I even put
'em in that."

"Well you done set my head to spinning.
You may need to go with me, and let's find
this together. I will hitch up Maude. You get
the children, and we will make a day of it. I'll
take my gun, and maybe I'll shoot something
for you to cook with them ramps."

"We can do that. I can teach you all about
making do in these mountains. I am pretty sure
you have never had to do that before. Not
ever."

"We weren't rich by anybody's thoughts,
but we did always have plenty to eat. But I'm
not above doing what we have to do to fill a
gut.

Her laughter filled the room and felt like a
warm blanket on a cold day. The children

started to laugh too. Who would've thought that talking about being poor could make us laugh?

"You surprise me, Nathe Milsaps. A person would think you would hightail it out of these mountains if it meant that we had to hunt for every morsel of food we get to eat. But you have not put me down or made fun of me for wanting to make it on my own with my children. I thank ye for that.

"I will get my bonnet in case the sun comes out, and a quilt in case Clare decides to sleep on the way back home."

xxx

I took to hunting early every other morning for small game. I left the meat with Addie to cook. The children's mouth watered every time I brought in a squirrel or rabbit. Come the end of week, I planned to hunt up on the mountain near my home place and try to get a deer. Addie and I would strip it out and make jerky for those times when it got too busy for me to bring in any meat. Good jerky could last through the year and be relied upon to stave off hunger, if other food supply ran out. My time of freedom after that fun day of being together like a family was over, and the work in the fields was from sunup to sundown.

xxx

The rain had sent gulley-washers during the night but had slowed to a foggy mist and spattering of sprinkles since daylight. The fields were too wet to plow or plant. It was going to be a rainy, wet spring. There was still plenty to do.

If it was one thing that Jonathan taught me before he went to war, it was how to work without supervision. Thank the Lord for that. Addie's sixty acres showed the results of no man around. The only fields that were still tetotally cleared were the corn field and the garden. And those were obviously smaller than before, showing the fact that a woman and small boy had to work the field and garden. Evidently, when Ashe was there, he had pastured about twenty acres, had a hay field, and another small clearing for cotton. It would be only enough cotton for the family to use for spinning and making cloth. Maybe a smidgen more. One season of cotton was all he had harvested before the war. All of the fields were being taken over by eight to ten year old hardwoods and young saplings, a few as big around as my arm.

Davie stayed at the house to water the horse and cut some grass for Maude to eat.

In the light rain, I cut saplings from what I hoped would be a corn field and piled them to use for mending fences. I used a sickle on the blackberry briers that had taken over the pasture. There would be plenty of other berries growing by the road to use for canning when

the time came. With any luck, in another
week, there would be enough land cleared to
have a cow or two if she wanted them, and if
she could find a way to pay for them. Someone
at the store might know if there was one that
could be purchased. I might be able to swing
the cost of one as partial pay for my keep and
have some fresh milk and butter. There was a
pen for hogs near the roadside about a quarter
mile up the road. Hopefully there would be
enough saplings to mend that as well. The
purchase of a hog would have to be later.
Maybe next year. It would have to be killed in
the winter and salted and cured to make it last.
I would be long gone. She would probably
find a good man to marry, and he could help
her. Just thinking about that made my stomach
feel queasy.

If it was still too wet to plow on the
morrow, I planned to use Maude to pull out the
smaller stumps. I would pile them on a stump
left in the ground from a bigger tree, and burn
them.

xxx

The work day ended when a strong storm
came out of the west and ran me to the house.
Addie and the children were sitting on the
porch waiting for me when I came in.

"You are soaking wet. Do you have extra
clothes that you can change into?"

"I sent them here to the house for Friday's washing. I will sit in the barn until I dry."

"No you will not. I have some clothes of Ashe's in the bedroom. I will get you a change. I kept 'em to cut down for Davie as he grows. You stand right here on the porch till I come back."

Davie wiped his hands on his breeches. "I took care of Maude. I pulled grass for a long time. I took bresh and made me a pallet to pile the grass on. Then I brought it to the barn and put it in the loft in piles."

I smiled at his ability to build a make-shift skidder to bring in the grass. "Let me see those hands." He stuck them out with his palms up. "There are grass cuts all over your hands. Has yore mamma seen these? You need to have meat grease rubbed on them. Does it hurt bad?"

"A little. It mostly stings."

I pulled him into my arms and saw a pool of tears gather at the bottom of his eyes. He swallowed hard and looked at the sky. "Do you think this rain will last long?" He tried to occupy his mind with something other than the pain.

"Maybe. At least long enough for us to catch our breath." I took a rag and wet it. As I patted the red scratches, he winced and rocked back and forth trying not to cry out loud.

He's just a little boy. I wish he could live like the child he is and not have to work so hard. His little body was bony and thin. At first he resisted when I pulled him on my knee. He turned red and put his back to me. I made like a horse galloping and got Clare on my knee to ride while Davie sat still on the other.

"Ok, Clare girl, its Davie's turn." Davie laughed and held to my knee. He beat the side of his leg with his hand like he was riding free through a valley. There are not many carefree moments in a boy's life that loses his papa at so early an age. He had to be the man of the house. It was a rare time of being a child, and he laughed so hard he cried. I got to enjoy it with him, and I'll never forget that. I wondered if he would remember this time when he was all grown up. I hoped so.

My clothes were no longer dripping, and I went into the house. She had laid out baby clothes and other things she wanted to keep. There were tears in her eyes. Addie had gotten to Ashe's clothes. Remembering. She rose and handed me a shirt and breeches. "I know this is a white, Sunday-go-to-meeting shirt, but it will be fine for today. These breeches were the last ones I sewed before he left to fight in the war. I think he only wore them one time. He left them thinking they would be nice for when he came back, and he could use them for Sunday clothes."

"This is too nice for me to get dirty."

"Just do jobs that are not so dirty until I get the clothes washed. I put two barrels under the edge of the house last night and caught rain water for washing. I've got some lye soap, and

I'll wash them now and bring them to you. You can hang them in the barn to dry. Not much else we can do outside with the rain so heavy."

"I'll be careful with these nice clothes."

"I don't have no need for them unless I cut them down to make Davie something. I wanted to bury Ashe in them, but his body never came home."

The search in the trunk made her want to talk about her memories. "He died at Cumberland Gap, but they never did find his body. Someone saw him get shot and said he was bleeding all over the place. Next thing they knew, he was gone. No one ever saw him again. They was sure he was wounded unto death. It would have been good to say goodbye. Even to know there was a grave somewhere that I might see someday. To know that he had a decent place of rest, not just left to the animals to devour."

She took her apron and dabbed at her eyes. "Here I am a going on and on, and you shivering from those wet clothes. The wind is blowing cold air again. You will catch your death of cold. Hope this don't bring freezing temperatures. Git on out of here."

"I'll go to the barn and change."

The clothes fit well exceptin' the sleeves were a little short. I rolled them up a ways and made it look better.

There was a barrel in the tack room that I had noticed the day I came. I wanted to see what was in it, but it seemed there was never enough time for snooping. That was exactly what it was, I know, but I consoled myself saying there might be something that could be used.

The barrel had wooden staves of white oak bound with a metal band at top and bottom. There was a thick wooden slab from a white oak tree nailed to the top. It took some doing, but I got the top off and found it packed with raw cotton.

Addie will be surprised and happy. There was a spinning wheel in the corn crib. I had seen it the other day when I swept the building out. There was a wooden well bucket alongside it with a hand carder and a hand spindle in it. It looked in good repair except the treadle was loose. I nailed the lid back on.

I twisted and turned the barrel and walked it to the house. I would have turned it over and rolled it, but the mud would have seeped between the staves and made the cotton stained and knotty.

Addie heard me trying to get it on the porch. "Where did you get that? What is in that barrel, and why are bringing it to the house?"

"You don't' know? It was in your barn."

"I wouldn't be asking if I did. Where did you find it?"

"In the tack room. Back in a corner." I knocked off the lid again and watched her face.

"Cotton." She pulled up hands full and put it next to her face. "This is cotton, Nathe. I can make thread to sew with. I can dye it and weave it and make cloth. Where did you say you got it?"

I wasn't sure I could talk with the lump in my throat the size of a fist. "The barn…in the tack room."

"Why have I never seen it? I don't know when it could have been put there. Or who did it. We had a field of cotton one year, but it didn't do all that well. And Ashe was gone the next. Whose do you suppose it is?"

"It's in yore barn, so I suppose it's yores."

"Do you really think it is mine? That I can use it?"

"Yep. This is yore barn. If somebody else stored it there, surely they would have come back for it or let you know that it was there. So as I see it, it is yorn. There is a hand spindle in the corn crib. Do you want me to get it?"

"I knew that was there. Just had no reason to have it in the house. But, no. Don't get it yet. This is raw cotton, and we need to get the seeds out. We can use those seeds too, can't we? Find us a field to plant them and have more cotton."

"Well not this year. There's no time to get cotton planted with all we got to do, and another field would have to be cleared."

Her laughter rang out as she raised her hands to the sky. "Thank you God for rain right now. This day. Finding these blessings

You hid just for this time. Amen. Have a seat
boys, We are going to pull seeds out of the
cotton. It's a rainy day job. Come on Clare.
Even you can do this work."

Chapter 8

The sun set behind the mountain making the sky and clouds a dusky gray. The mountains turned a bluish haze with shadows that hid the valleys and made them look like one large mountain. I opened the doors of the loft and sat on the edge with my feet dangling. Addie would soon have supper, but until then I needed to catch my breath. There were days when my mind was so full with all the work to do that I didn't have time to think of my plan to revenge. I could not let that happen. It's all about remembering, Papa said. He drove that into my mind for nine years. I heard it almost every week of those years.   It had to be kept alive inside me.

The work here was hard with no pay. It would never help me get enough money to pay for a place of my own. But I had to tell myself that, if I would bide my time, when the crops were laid by, there would be time and opportunity to destroy every person responsible for my family's deaths. And maybe their families too. That would be pay a plenty. Now to plant, plow, and lay by the fields. While the crops and garden grew, I would search.

In the house, there was laughter.   Addie picked up Clare and held her in her lap. She rocked her in the rocker that her mother had rocked Addie when she was a baby.

As I grew up, I never thought about what would happen beyond the time when I would come back and take my revenge. But seeing Addie and the children made me wonder what my life would be like when I could settle down. Of course, I might not live to do that. There was the possibility I could die in my attempts. What if the feud had never started? What would my life have been like? It had been hard to picture myself with a wife or children before I came here. Today it seemed like a good way of life. But it was not my life. Things for me were different. *Don't forget why you're here. Quit thinking about this family and get down to business.* A man has to talk to himself at times.

I pulled out a piece of brown paper from my bag. It was worn, and what I had written had grown dim. But I could still read it, and that was all that mattered. Soon after arriving at Jonathan's and Jemena's, I wrote down the name of every man that had come into our house to do us harm. I'm not sure if I thought I would forget their names. It would not have been possible, even if I tried. Not the least because I heard Mama, Papa, and Tercy screaming their names in my dreams. Their faces were burned in my memory, as though it were yesterday. Of course, they would have aged. Ten years in these mountains could change a young man to an old one with its harsh life. Would it be enough that I wouldn't recognize them?

Only one time did I mention the particulars of that night to Jemena. I told her the story revealing every detail I remembered, and I showed her my list. She told me she never wanted me to talk or think about that again. She made me promise to throw that paper away. It was the only real lie I can remember telling Jemena. As for the paper with their names on it, well it never saw the light of day again, unless I was by myself. The list told things that might be done to each Hooper on that list. Shoot 'em. Tie them in a chair and beat them to death. Hang 'em from a tree in their own yard. As I grew older, the list got more detailed. If the men were dead, then their children had to pay. The plans was well

formed in my mind. The first thing was to
hunt them down and find out everything about
them that I could. Carefully, of course. That
meant that I had to cautiously mingle among
the families on these mountains. The plan had
always been to find my family. Then the
Watsons would go to a Hooper's home, like
they did mine and take care of the matter. I
never dreamt that my family would not join
me when push came to shove. But it occurred
to me now that Corsie and Linny might not
help or allow any of their children to join me.
My visit with Linny hadn't been profitable.
Corsie was next. Maybe she would be of a
different frame of mind. Papa, Monroe, and
Robert would have been fit to be tied if they
knew his family had fallen apart and didn't do
anything about their deaths. I wanted to pull
our family back together.

xxx

The first day in Jackson County, as I had
passed Aunt Corsie's house, there had been
smoke billowing from the chimney, so I knew
someone lived there. *I wish I had asked Aunt
Linny about her.*

Today, I knocked on the door, and it was
answered by a girl of about fourteen. I hadn't
remembered they had a daughter. There were
six boys. I forgot the seventh was a girl. She
would have been about four when I left.

"Hello, ma'am. Someone told me that a Miss Corsie might be a-needing some work done."

"Well, mister, they lied. If we needed work to be done, I have brothers in these parts to do it. Or better yet, I would have done it."

So there are some other Watsons still here. All had not moved away, or died.

"What are you smiling at? You think I can't do any work she needs? If a man can do it, I can do it. I can even wipe that grin off your face. Or better, I can shoot it off." She reached for a gun that stood next to the door.

I saw a stooped figure make her way toward the door behind the young girl.

"Eliza, get your hands off that gun. Who's at the door?"

She turned toward her mother. "Some lying stranger. He thinks we need a hand in the fields. Said somebody told him that." She turned back and pointed her finger in my face. "If somebody told you that, you just go back and tell them they lied. Do you hear me? They're liars."

"Hush now Eliza. Let me see this man."

Corsie pushed past Eliza, put the back of her hands on her hips, and looked me from crown to toe. She pursed her lips and spit tobacco on the dirt at my feet. "I think the man might need a drink of water, Eliza. Run to the spring and get a fresh bucket."

"He don't need no drink. If he does, he can get it on his way out.'

"Do you hear me, girl? Get your butt up to that spring."

"But mama, I ain't leaving you alone with a stranger."

"Yes you are. You're going to do what you're told to do. Get that bucket and head on to the spring, I said."

Eliza eyed me with hate. I could not help but smile. Only a true Watson could be as suspicious and hateful as she was. She grabbed the bucket and swung it. She purposely hit my arm as she passed by me. "You better not touch my mama, do you hear me? If you do, I will claw your eyes out."

"Yes ma'am."

She left running toward the spring that was about a quarter mile up the road.

"Somebody said I needed a hand to work for me, huh? You look like a Watson, but you don't sound like one. A Watson might do a lot of things, but he don't usually lie. Get in here, boy. You're Nathe, am I right?"

"Yes ma'am, but how did you know?"

"Hmp. Linny whispered to me a few days ago that you was around. But I could have picked you out in a room full of men. You have your daddy's eyes and your mama's round face. Eliza don't know. That's why I sent her packing until we could talk."

"How are you, Aunt Corsie?"

"Well finer than most people think. They all believe I am a crazy as a Bessie bug. And I just let them think it. I know better, and that is all that matters. It makes them leave me alone, and I leave them alone."

She shook her head from side to side. "It's too dangerous for you to be living around here, or even passing through. And it's way too risky for you to be coming to my house."

"I had to see you at least once, Aunt Corsie. Do any of your sons live around here?"

"Why are you asking that? You don't need to be visiting any of them, either. They think you're dead."

"They're my cousins. It's only natural I would want to visit them. We always was a close family."

Her eyes narrowed, and she pursed her lips again. She grabbed a fruit jar filled with what looked like hay or grass and spit dark brown juice into it. She pulled her lips out like she was going to kiss something and rolled them round. A large plug of chewing tobacco dropped into the jar.

"If you have any thinking going on in that head of yours about starting up the feud again, you just get it out of there. I made my boys sign a paper after their papa's funeral. They promised the feud stopped with the death of my husband, your daddy, and the others."

Well, that was waste of paper and ink. If they cared about their daddy, that is. They were Watsons and would say whatever their mama wanted them to say, even if they didn't mean it. Because a Watson took care of matters. They stood up for family before anything. "I don't know what you are talking about."

"Sure you do. And I'm shore your mama would want me to turn your bottom end up and give you the whooping of your life, if you even think about such a thing. I don't know what you got in your head over in Tennessee, but I am truthful in saying my boys have left the feud behind them. Those Hoopers are not worth killing. Let them rot here and in hell."

Eliza came in, and Corsie looked into the bucket. "Lorda mercy, girl. Did you even try to fill it up? You done spilled it all but a sup."

She took the bucket from her daughter and handed it to me. "Try to slake your thirst with what little water she got back with, stranger. But we don't need any help right now. Not much work in these mountains. We're poorer than Job's turkey and could not afford to pay a body to work anyways." Her eyes stared into mine like two balls of fire.

"Yes ma'am. Then I'll be on my way."

I looked back one last time to see Eliza watching me. She narrowed her eyes and spit at me. I laughed out loud.

"Git out of here, and don't you be coming back in these mountains, stranger. Heads have rolled for lesser things." She laughed back at me.

I wished the men of this family had a single flame of the fire that she had and half the backbone. If they had, we could take care of this in a few days.

Chapter 9

The dirt was hardened from the heavy spring rains, and the clumps felt like rocks. It was the third time I had gone over the garden trying to break the clods of dirt. I would turn-up about one-third of the garden now for the root crops and the rest later. It didn't hope matters that all Addie had was a wooden plow. Jemena's husband had a new metal plow that I got to use before leaving Tennessee. It was a grand thing. It could've cut right through the hard ground. What a help it would be if I had one right now. *If wishes was gold, I could buy this mountain **and** a steel plow.*

Addie sat at the end of the row cutting eyes from the seed potatoes. She yelled to me above the scraping of the plow. "There should be enough of the potato eyes for about twelve good size rows."

The strength of the ground looked rich and prosperous. In a few weeks, we could grabble out a few tiny potatoes to put in some peas, then add some dumplings. The harvest should be full grown in about four months.

I took the next section to break up the ground all over again. The hard, packed dirt jerked the plow from my hands and made my teeth hurt from the shaking. I put my whole weight into the plow handles, pushing it down until my feet left the ground. After the clods were fully broken up, I laid off enough rows for some English peas. She hadn't said what else she needed to plant today, but there should be plenty of room for it. There were a few more daylight hours we could work.

"Guess you didn't think to look to see what the signs were for planting did you?"

My face turned bright red. "Jem…Mama always checked the signs, so I didn't think about it."

"Well I did, and the Farmer's almanac says the moon is darkening. That makes it a good time. It should be a dark night tonight. Next week, the signs are in the feet, and that would be too late. Those potatoes would have little toes all over them, if we planted them then."

"Well, as I always told Mama, when you have good help seems like to me would be when the signs is the best."

Addie picked up a small clod of dirt and threw it. It barely missed my right shoulder.

Davie and Addie dropped the potato eyes into the ground about ten inches apart and finished covering them with about five inches of dirt with the hoe. Clare sat in the shade a little ways from the garden and played with her doll, making mud pies and playing house. She didn't have many play purties from what I could tell. But she shore seemed to love that doll I had made her. I needed to think what all my sister played with as play purties.

Addie called to Davie, "Come to the end with your hoe and make me a little bed for some radishes. They'd be root crops, and the signs will be fine for them too."

She unwrapped a small cloth and carefully spread out tiny radish seeds. She took a pinch to sow in the rows she had made with her little finger. She took soil from the ends and covered them with about a half-inch of dirt.

"I found these in my seeds I had stored in a barrel in the corncrib. They should still be good, even though I have had them a few years. Can you take a stick and pull me long row to the side for some carrots? Just drop the reins on Maude. She'll stand there. "

I made the rows about a quarter inch deep, and she was right behind me dropping the carrot seeds about two inches apart and covered them with her toes as she went.

"I wish I lived closer to Mama. She would have some cabbage sets for me. I should have planted me cabbage seeds weeks ago, and I would have had my own plants. Now it's too late. Sure do hate that. I have got to learn to think ahead. Mama won't always be around for me to depend on."

We had started just after breakfast, and now the sun was straight above us. At the end of the row, I rolled my shirt sleeves up to just above my elbows. When I looked up, Addie was watching me. She quickly picked up the edge of the apron she was wearing and wiped the sweat from her face. She dropped her apron and used her finger tips to push loose strands of hair back into the bun at the top of her head. I had never seen her hair down, and I really wanted to. There was a lot of hair in that bun so it must reach clear to her waist.

Addie looked away from my gaze and stared at Clare as she spoke to me. "You go ahead and take Maude up to the barn and water her. I'll take the children and see if those beans I left cooking are done. I will cut up that dab of cornbread I cooked this morning, and we can eat dinner."

I carried water from the pond that was below the barn and filled the wooden trough. Maude drunk most of the water, and I refilled it. I left the harness on her for the time being.

At the house, Addie sliced the cornbread and divided it in half, the rest to be eaten at supper. She had taken some of the potatoes she had cut the eyes from, chopped them, and fried them in some lard, along with chopped up shallots.

She handed a jar to me. "Open it, if you don't care. It's the last jar of my pickled okra and onions. Okra was plentiful last year, and people at church brought me bushels of it. I pickled as much as I could. The kids got to hate the sight of them because that was all we had to eat a few weeks ago. Until the church gave us some food. Sure glad we are getting the garden out. Feeding an extra person these past few weeks has taken its toll on the food supply."

"I'm sorry about that."

"Don't be sorry. You are helping us plant the best and most varied vegetable garden we've had in years. If the good Lord gives us the increase of our work today, it'll be the biggest harvest in ages, and we'll eat good next winter as well as all this summer. You've more than paid for your keep, Nathe Milsaps. I don't begrude a bite you've eaten. I was just thinking that it takes a family putting up a lot of food to make it in life."

Her words warmed me inside. I felt needed and appreciated. "When dinner is over, I think I will work on the field I cleared. I can start digging out stumps and plowing. I think that field would be good for a field of corn. If I have to, I will plant and plow around most of the stumps."

"That's a fine idea. You can always dig them up after harvest and before the ground gets too frozen. I can even help you…"

She blushed deep red when she saw my face. "I'm sorry. You'll probably have moved on by then. I was just talking and not using the wisdom God gave me. It's just easy to think you are here to stay, I reckon. Don't hold it against me. I understand our agreement."

I didn't know what to say, so I ignored it. "That field up by the spring would make a good field for sugar cane. This year, I mean."

"Sugar cane. It's been ages since we had us any good sugar cane. Molasses. That makes fine cookies and cakes. Papa has a molasses mill. He will make it for us."

Davie and Clare jumped up and down at the mention of molasses and day dreamed about lassy tea cakes, like any child would. I grabbed Clare and threw her in the air and caught her. She grabbed my neck and hugged me.

"I love 'lassy cakes," she squealed.

Addie reached for Clare. She stooped and gave her a hug. "So do I, baby girl. I love molasses in lots of things. Mama gives me some along, but it is only enough for breakfast occasionally. And the preacher gave us some, but all of its gone. But to have our own supply, that would be like heaven here on earth. I will try to save a few eggs to sell and see if I can buy the seed for that field of sugar cane. If I had a cow giving a good amount of milk, and if I made some extra butter, I could sell that too. Or trade it for seeds. But here I am daydreaming again. If pigs had wings, they could fly. What's the matter with me? I am no earthly good when I get like this."

She was as excited as the children. I wanted to buy those things for her. Seeing her with a hope for a better life made me feel happy, as happy as I had been in many a year.

Chapter 10

The winds turned from the north again. It was blackberry winter, one of several types of weather spells that hit the mountains as spring tried to descend on us. Planting, for the time being, was set aside. We were glad that at least the potatoes, peas, and few other root crops were in the ground. I used the time of colder weather to work on the barn and the wagon. The wagon wheel was in need of repair. Something I didn't have the tools or the know-how to fix. It required a visit to Speedwell to find someone that could do it.

My trip took me by Amp's place, so I decided to look for him. *I wonder if he owns the house and land where he's staying.* You'd think he'd try to fix up the house instead of living out in the weather. He didn't look like the gypsies I'd seen over the years passing through with wagons and potions to sell. Most every time, Amps had stood by that fire.

Below the house, Greasy Creek sat low in a gulley, and the water rushed over rocks and fallen trees. I could make out his head and shoulders walking by the stream. He appeared to glide along, moving without effort over the rocks by the river. His body never moving up and down as a person normally would. The man gave me the willies. He looked up the hill and saw me and came to where I stood.

I enjoyed my talks with him, though I was unsure why. He appeared to know much more about me than I knew about him. It was a mystery how he knew. Amps seemed to look deep into my soul and know my thoughts. I should have taken this as a warning to stay away. He was strange. He never mentioned friends or going to church. I didn't really think he was a Hooper, and there wasn't a Watson I remembered that looked like him. This land, with the house and barn where he was staying, once belonged to my grandpa. He had died before I was born. Maybe it would be possible to find out who bought it. Maybe at the church. Aunt Corsie's words echoed. 'Don't be asking too many questions.'

Speaking of church, I probably should go again. Several weeks had passed, and I didn't think Jemena would call it regular church attendance. I would dress up as best I could and bring the wagon around. Addie and the children would see I was dressed for Sunday go to meeting. Hopefully, they would not think about the fact I had not gone for some time.

At the church, I could ask names of people without sounding suspicious. They would expect me to try to get to know people. And I could look at Addie all dressed up in that nice dress she saved for church. I caught a glimpse of her early last Sunday morning after I had hitched up the wagon and brought it up to the house. She was a pretty woman. I wonder if she would be embarrassed if I asked to attend the house of God with her. Ride in the wagon alongside the family. She might not want to get tongues a wagging like they would if we came together. One day I would ask her. She seemed always to be in my thoughts.

Amps threw up his hand in recognition. "Good morning to you, Nathe. Where are you heading?"

I untied the rope that held the wagon wheel on my back. I sat it on the ground and rubbed my shoulder. "Going to find a place to get the wheel fixed. There are two spindles missing. I'm scared that Miss Addie and the children might have trouble on some Sunday if this is not taken care of. I can see that wheel hub breaking if it gets caught in a hardened rut. The wheel might slip into one and twist. Too dangerous for a woman and children. Don't rightly know where to go to have it fixed, but figured I would find someone. Maybe check at the store down in East LaPorte."

'Why not try Mill's Blacksmith Shop. I hear tell that a man named John Mills has a foot-pedal lathe. He could put out new spindles in a short time."

Amps gave me directions.

"It's right kindly of you to think about that family like that. I thought you were just doing farm work. But you seem to be taking care of that widow woman well."

"Where did you hear that I was staying at a widow woman's house?"

"Word gets around in these mountains. I told you that."

"I'm just working for room and board. She's a fine woman. It would be a poor excuse for a man that would leave a woman to the prey of these mountains when there was something that he could fix or get fixed. I wouldn't be worth my salt as man to hire if I was like that. But I want you to know, she is a fine upstanding woman."

He left off talking about my boarding at Addie's. "You must have a mighty fine papa to teach you things like how to treat a lady. He must be a kindhearted and honorable man."

Blood rushed into my face, and I looked away. Papa never taught me that. Jemena taught me kindness. I tried to recall things that my real Papa had taught me. There was the whittling. That was a thing of honor. I needed to whittle a toy or something for Davie. I had yet to see him play with anything. He was like an old man in a little boy's body. He had been the man of the house for most of his life. Too much for a boy to carry. I should know.

My Papa had taught me to shoot a gun and how to field dress a deer and skin a squirrel. Hunting food for the family was honorable. He taught me that family was important, that you stick together and defend each other to the death.

"My papa was a good man. He's been gone a few years now."

"Sorry to hear that. You must have been young when he died."

"Fairly young." I nodded my head at him and tied the wheel back onto my back. To have to buy and pay for a whole wheel, if it skittled its way down the mountain side, was more than I could afford.   It would cost enough to get spindles.

Before I had gone a hop and a skip, I realized that Amps was walking behind me.

"Where are you going Amps?"

"Thought I might take a walk down to the Tuckasegee. I will walk with you on your way to East LaPorte. Maybe fish a little." He carried nothing in his hands. " So, are you thinking of settling down here in North Carolina?"

"Still undecided. It is nice. I have met some good people."

"The widow woman you're living with must be a good cook. You have fleshened up a bit. Kind of pooching out in your belly."

"I am living in the barn." I patted my stomach. "Nothing to complain about in her cooking. Never tasted better. But doubt that I'm any heavier. Not with all the work I've been doing and the lack of food in the house. You're a pretty close neighbor. Did you know she was almost starving to death up there?"

"I don't get out much, I told you. Besides I don't have much myself. Mostly meat that I kill or some roots that I dig to make a soup."

I remembered that Amps never wore a coat, even in the coldest of weather. I was ashamed that I had spoken such to him. He didn't seem to have much in the way of worldly goods. The house was not in good enough repair for living. The barn was not much better.

Acorn tops were scattered across the road, the nut part long since eaten by deer or squirrels or some other varmint. I reached down and picked up a top. That's what a person does when they make a fool of themselves. They change the subject.

"What you doing, boy?"

"Addie's girl, Clare, would love to play with these like cups. My sister used to do that when we were young. I made Clare a cornshuck doll, and now she can have tea with her. These can be little plates and cups."

"You sound like you are settling in to be a family man."

"They's not my family, blood wise, but I feel responsible for them. Jemen…my mother taught me to be kind and think about others, and it just comes natural I guess. That woman and those kids work hard to make ends meet. This year might be a little better with me living in the barn and helping out. And, likewise, I've had a place to stay and food to eat."

Amps picked up a stick and balanced himself against it. He looked feeble and tired.

"But I don't want you thinking hard of her. She's a fine, honorable woman. I don't want no wagging tongues making her out to be a loose woman. If they do, you and them will have me to deal with."

He nodded, but the smile on his face made me madder than a wet hen. I wished he would go back to his fire.

Being he was set on walking with me, I had a few questions he might clear up. "Amps, you live around here. Why have I not seen Addie's mama and papa? I know they live a little piece from here but close enough I would think to visit."

"Have you asked her why they've not been around? Especially with all her needs.

She could have used their help, don't you think?"

"I don't really think she would feel kindly of me asking. I am just a hired hand. It's not any of my business. There's not really a reason for me to meet them, I guess. She did tell me they lived a ways from here."

Amps did not breathe hard at all, but I could barely catch my breath.

"I hear that her papa is not well. Could be they can't make the trip, although, if she was my daughter, I would at least make the effort. It sounds like Addie is too busy to go there. Think her family lives over in the direction of Cashiers now. Their son lives close to them I think. The land the widder's house is on was her papa's place. It was burned to the ground once by somebody, so they moved on."

"Thank ye for the information. I try not to be a busybody and ask lots of questions. I don't know many people to ask. Come to think of it, you are as near to a friend as I have in these parts. Unless you count the preacher that told me to ask Addie about helping out at her place."

"Glad you think of me as a friend. Ain't had a friend myself in many a year."

It was a mystery to me why I even said friend. I knew nothing about him. Just the fact that he showed up when I had questions or wanted to know something made it seem like he was a friend, I guess. I left Amps at a footlog that I took over the Tuckasegee. I could hear him whistling a tune as I walked away, and he headed up the river.

xxx

As I passed the general store in East Laporte on the way to the blacksmith shop, I saw cabbage sets on the front steps. There wasn't a lot of money in my possession but hoped I had enough to get some for Addie. I reached in my pocket, pulled it out, and counted it.

When Jemena married, they planned to sell her place and move to her new husband's farm. The chickens she took with her, but they had given me two cows, the horse, and two sows, which I sold. I wish I had ridden the horse over here but did not know how long I would have to live without finding work, so I sold her. If I was careful, the money could last until my job here was done and I was on my way. Maybe even set me up in some town midways in the state of Tennessee or up in Virginia.

I would stop back for the plants on my way home from the blacksmith and buy what we needed. It wasn't like it was all for Addie. I had to eat too.

I took the wheel off my shoulder and rolled it into the blacksmith shop that Amps had suggested.

The man took the horseshoe he had been beating on the anvil with a pair of iron tongs and stuck it into the water.

"I have this wheel that needs two spokes. I hear tell you have a foot lathe that would make quick work of fixing the wheel I got."

"You heard the truth. I can fix it."

The voice had a deep, throaty sound, almost familiar. I looked into his face begging myself to remember.

"I can see that you do not know who I am."

My hands shook, and I laid the wheel against the door. Was it a Hooper? The skin was darker than any of them. Most Hoopers were fair complected and freckled. This man might have been borned with dark skin, or he could be just weather worn. It was hard to tell.

"Nathe, it's me. Inola." He pushed out his hand to me.

Inola. My Indian friend. I grabbed his hand and pulled him into my arms. "I thought I would never see you again. I realize now your voice sounds like your papa's."

He slapped me on the back. "I thought you were dead or long since gone. Thought I would never see you again."

Our eyes looked at each other from head to toe and remembered days gone by. He was grown. Gone were the fat little cheeks and the dark braids. Now his face was lean and his hair short. The ten-year old boy was now a strong young man.

"I heard tell about those that killed Mr. Watson and the others. It was a terrible thing to happen. I watched outside the graveyard the day they were buried. It would not have been good for me to go, father said. They told that you saw everything that happened. When I did not see you again, I thought they had gotten you too, but everyone was too scared to say it."

I looked around to make sure we were alone. "Inola, I don't want anyone to know I'm back. It could be dangerous. It's true that I saw them kill my family. I know them all by name."

"You must be careful. Why would you come back?"

I wondered if he could understand how important it was for me to even out the wrong to my family. He had once talked to me about the Cherokee loyalty to family. Surely he would know. It would take time to find out if he could still be trusted.

"Do you work at this mill?"

"I own the mill."

"They told me a John Mills owned it."

"I am John Mills. I married Synthee Mills and we thought it best that, since I had pale skin for an Indian and could be mistaken for a dark complected white man, we use her family name as ours. Inola isn't a common white man's name, so we use John. The Mills lived just over the mountain from us, and I fell in love with Synthee. Her father came to live for two years on the reservation and was paid to teach blacksmithing. All those years of whittling with you and your papa made me

love to work with wood, and blacksmithing
was a job that let me use metal and wood to
make things. I became an apprentice to
Synthee's papa. When Mr. Mills left the
reservation, he came and built the blacksmith
shop. Synthee and I married a month later. We
came here, and I worked for him. Now I own
it. I have bellows, anvil, vise, a screwplate,
hammers and rasps, and a half dozen or more
hasps and files. Last month I bought this foot
pedal lathe from a traveling salesman from the
North. He sent it on a train to the other side of
Sylva, and I picked it up. It has taken me some
time to learn to use it, but I'm pretty good at it
now, if I do say so myself. Synthee thinks it's
good work. I have done well."

"You are married. What a surprise." I
slapped him on the back, and he laughed.

"Life will be better now that you are here
my friend."

My smiled faded. "It is best for now that
you don't tell anyone that you know me or
who I am. I'm alarmed that you recognized
me. Although I'm glad too." I nodded and
smiled. "You're right. I fear that I might not be
long on the earth if they find I'm here."

"Tell me, friend, why did you come
back?"

"It is a long story. Someday I will tell you.
But it's best you know nothing for the time
being."

Inola looked alarmed. "Don't do anything
foolish, Nathe. It was ages ago, and it's best if

you don't bring it into this day. No good can
come of bringing it back up."

"The wheel. How quick can you fix it?"

He stepped backward and looked hurt.
"The wheel can be fixed in a couple of hours.
If you can find something to do nearby and
come back, or you may leave it and pick it up
tomorrow."

"I saw some things down at the store that I
need. I'll be back to pick it up in two hours."

"Very well. See you then." His brows
were drawn together, and his eyes looked
wounded.

My heart wanted to trust him, but
something would not let me depend on
anyone. Not yet. "Be patient, Inola. John. I'll
tell you some time." He nodded but still
looked worried.

xxx

"How much are your cabbage sets on the
porch?"

With the price he quoted, I could afford
enough sets for several rows. Boiled cabbage
now and kraut for the winter. My mouth
watered. Inside were rows of metal bins with
all kinds of seeds. If only I'd asked her what
seeds she had saved for planting and then I'd
know what I should buy. The ones that caught
my eyes were watermelon and mushmelons.
Those grew well on the land on Little Pigeon
River in Tennessee. Mmmm. How sweet they

were to eat on a hot August afternoon. Just pull them from the vine and put them under the front porch in the shade for about two days and they would be fine eating. Davie and Clare would be so happy. Shoot, me and Addie would be plum happy, too.

"There are some pepper plants too, if you'd like any."

I picked out about twenty plants of peppers, hot and sweet. Those could be pickled when their time came and would be good winter eating.

Men sat around a dying fire, swapping lies and bragging about their hunting dogs. They paid no mind to me, and I searched their faces for signs of a Hooper.

A man with large, muscled arms and a rounded belly came in and sat down with the others. "My boy is getting hitched next month to Absalom Wilson's daughter. I was hoping to help him find a farm. I came down here today to see if any of you know anyone that is wanting to sell."

"Not much anyone moving in or out of this here area, Elliott. You know that."

"I heard that Corsie Watson was poorly, and her place might come up for sale." The speaker took two fingers and divided them, placing one to each side of his lips. He spit tobacco juice between them into the coals of the fire then wiped his fingers on his pants.

"I thought she died years ago."

"She's still in the land of the living. She shares a reasonable portion of health in body, but her mind leaves a lot to be desired."

Everyone laughed. It made me angry, the way they were speaking about her with no respect.

"If she dies, that young wildcat daughter of hers can't take care of the land. Unless one of you has a son that is willing to take her on."

"There ain't no boy that could take her on. I heard tell she could win a wrestling match with a bear."

I moved to the keg of nails and out of earshot. It wouldn't do to let myself get worked up and fly off the handle. It was best to not listen. Eliza surely would be a handful, but their words felt too much like the thoughts the Hooper boys had toward Tersy and Rachel. And they were more than willing to take them on.

Leather for shoe soles and uppers hung by the counter. I had watched Jonathan make a pair of shoes for me the first year I was in Tennessee. After that, his Papa had made them. Clare or Davie Tom never wore shoes, even to church. Maybe I could make them each a pair. I bought the leather. There was that shoe last up at Aunt Linny's that I could use. There was an awl stuck in a crack in Addie's barn. I had seen it when I first arrived. I put a spool of strong cotton thread on the counter.

It took pretty much all the money I had on me. The rest was in my bag and hid in the barn loft. I was happy with my purchases. Hopefully, Addie would be pleased too. Behind the shoe leather, there hung the skin of a hog, two deer skins, and a bull hide. There was even skin from a rattlesnake and two beavers. Maybe I could kill some animals and skin them, then sell them for some money.

xxx

The wheel was ready when I returned. A young boy of about twelve tended the business, and Inola was nowhere to be seen.

"Where is Inol…..John?"

"He had to go to Synthee. The baby is coming. I am Synthee's little brother, Cling. He said to give it to you, and you could settle up later."

"Tell him thanks and that I will be back around to see him."

"Sure mister.

I hadn't given a thought about how I would get everything back up the mountain in one trip. It would've been good to have old Maude and the wagon. At the bottom of the mountain I piled fallen limbs and wove them to make a sled to pull behind me. I put the wheel on the top and propped up the plants between the spokes. I made the rope into a harness that I used on my mid parts and my shoulders and pulled the makeshift slide. It

was a drudgery but worth the effort when I
saw the smile on Addie's face.

Chapter 11

The rest of the garden plot was turned and raked smooth, ready to lay off in rows. Maude was harnessed and pawed at the ground ready to get on with the planting. I backed Maude up to the slide and hooked her up. The scoop went thud as it hit the wood when I threw it on the sled. The chickens pecked in the dirt, and didn't seem to mind that I was digging all the chicken manure out and piling it behind Maude to take to the garden. I would spread it with a pitchfork and take the turning plow to it again to mix it with the dirt.

"That smell ain't none too pleasant." Addie pinched her nose.

"No? Well we will see if it don't make those plants give a good increase and taste sumptuous." I threw a small pitchfork load toward her feet.

"Now stop that. I don't have no time to be washing clothes in order to have a dress to wear."

"I think it's all ready for planting."

"Well I am sure glad that you being ready to plant agrees with the Farmer's Almanac. Today it be in the loins, so everything we have here will grow good." She spoke with lots of conviction and faith in that book.

Addie clapped her hands. "I can hardly wait till these watermelons are ripe and we are eating them. It makes my mouth water."

"My mama always said 'don't be wishing your life away'."

"I'm not wishing life away. I am wishing watermelons would hurry up and get to where I am." She stuck her tongue out at me.

"You just never know what might happen between now and then." Mama always made me feel I was going make it happen by saying it.

"I thought you had no use for old sayings. You are no fun at all."

"As a rule, I don't believe those things, but this just seems true somehow. It seems that wishing for a day to end and another to hurry and get here is either a waste of time or asking for heartache. Sorry that you feel that I am no fun. Maybe soon we will make some time to have fun. But not today. It's planting time now. Got to get those watermelons to you as soon as they will grow."

She wrinkled her nose and pursed her lips out in a scowl. "Yes we do. And I forgive you. This time."

"Forgive me for what?"

"For making fun of my family. Especially as yores sounds just like mine."

xxx

Addie and the children were at church. It seemed plum lonesome when they were gone. I picked up my gun and walked toward the Watson place. Addie would not be happy with me hunting on Sunday, but I doubted she would turn down fresh meat if I brought any back for the week.

As I passed by, Amps was roasting what looked to be four rabbits on a stick across the fire.

"Well you went hunting early enough," I said.

"It's cooked, and some is ready to eat. Why don't you stay and have a bite with me. The two in the middle are done I be thinkin'. We can eat those, push the other two closer in, and they will be ready to eat by the time these are gone."

It smelled so good. "Thank you, Amps. I believe I will."

It was about the best rabbit I ever tasted. "How did you cook this? It's got some taste that's different from the way my mama cooked it."

Amps nodded his head toward a pot of water to his side as he gnawed on his piece of rabbit. "I parboil it with a pod or two of pickled hot pepper and a pinch of salt. Takes out that wild taste, and gives it some flavor."

While we waited for the other two rabbits to cook, Amps threw a stick of wood on the fire and sat down on a rotting log and tossed pine cones in the fire. I watched as he drained the sap from a green pine limb and let the liquid drip onto several pine cones. They could start a fire in no time flat.

I picked up my gun and rubbed it with my hands. My gun was the one possession I guarded close. It had been Papa's, and it was to be used for my plans. It would be like Papa was there with me.

"Amps, do you have family?"

"Yes, I have family. Most of the old ones are gone now. But in the mountains just about everyone is like family. We have to do that to survive. We raise barns and build houses. Harvest one another's crops, if sickness sets in, so the man's family will not starve." He stood and turned the stick that held the meat so it would cook all the way around.

"It doesn't sound that way when you talk about Hoopers and Watsons a-feuding. Sounds like they wouldn't help nobody."

"Well, that's true. That is why I tell you that this is no place for feuding. Maybe they found that out.

"I remember a Watson man went into the barn of a Hooper just after harvest. He burnt it to the ground along with the whole year's harvest inside. That poor family had nothing left to hope them through the winter. They were like paupers relying on the goodness of a few neighbors that could ill afford to share their meager harvest with another. But most of us here in the mountains would share as long as we got something to share and then starve to death together.

"So a Watson did that to a Hooper?" *Why have I never heard of this?*

"On yes. Neither family had many saints. The Watson man got hot and crazy. He failed to see what he didn't want to know." I stared blankly at Amps. "You know…that to try to get back at the Hoopers meant cutting your nose off to spite your face. It all comes back to haunt you. Especially with these families. He killed the only milk cow that the Hooper man owned. Back and forth for years. It may have been at one time about killing or destroying crops and animals, but it did not take long till it was damaging their women and on to murdering men. That dang founded war was just another excuse to shed blood."

"What exactly had that Hooper done that made a Watson want to do such a thing?" He acted like he did not hear me. "I suppose you and the rest of the country look down on the Hoopers and the Watsons."

"I know it sounds that way, and it would be understandable for that to be so. But I guess none of us are innocent in trying to avenge our pain…to want to make another feel the pain we have. We want to serve justice while the pain is still hot in our chest. We would be better to let it cool first. We feel undone until it is carried out."

Undone. Exactly. That is what I felt. Nothing would be right until they are reminded of the pain my mama felt when Papa died. Or some one of their women screaming with fear as their family member is pulled out of the house. No. I could not do that. But some father's child would cry their self to sleep because their daddy was murdered. In fact, they must be made to have it happen just like it happened to me. And I had not done it right after it happened. You would think the fire would have cooled in my heart and head, but it hadn't. If anything, it was hotter than ever.

Amps squeezed his eyes almost closed. "Son, a man must make sure he can live with the consequences of any actions he does. The devil will ride you hard all the way to the grave and afterwards."

I gritted my teeth. "The devil is a-working on both sides, when you kill, or when your family is the one dead. No escaping him is there?"

Amps moved his thumb from finger to finger, counting. "Out by the fire last night, I counted every Hooper and every Watson that I could remember that have died in these mountains at the hand of another. I just thought of another one. That makes twenty-five Hoopers and twenty-six Watsons."

I stood up and folded my arms. "Why are we talking about Hoopers and Watsons? Addie told me there has been many a man shot when he came upon a moonshine still and stayed long enough to have a look…even if he never took a drink. She never mentioned people of a certain name. Are the Hoopers and Watsons the only fighting people here?"

His coal-dark eyes squinted as he spoke. "Feuds, thievery, or whiskey killings. All have the same results. The death of the hope of a father for a son to carry on his name. A father trying to feed a family on the ashes of his harvest or the pity of his neighbors. A mother crying over the torn body of a daughter that will never bear a child or, worse, that she will never see full grown. It don't matter the name, be it Hooper, Watson, or Milsaps."

Amps reached behind the log nearby the fire and handed me the skins of the four rabbits. "You might want these for making something for those children. A winter glove or a poke to carry something in."

I tied the tails together and fastened them to my breeches. I picked up several rocks, walked to the edge of the water, and threw them one at time toward the other side. "I like you, Amps. You are purt near the only man I have talked to for any length of time since I have been here. But our conversations are sure strange."

"You are a good man, Nathe. But if you have come here for revenge, go ahead and dig two graves. You may walk away and breathe today. But you will walk as a dead man inside. It will destroy the very life you really want. To revenge makes you equal to the man or men that hurt you. To abstain from trying to get back, makes you better than him. You use your strength planning for the right time and the right place…energy that could be used to make a good life for you and yer children instead. "

I turned back to Amps. "I…" He was nowhere to be seen. The fire had burned down to a few coals, and there were bones of a rabbit piled neatly by the log where he had sat.

xxx

The day had gotten away fast, and I hadn't killed the deer that I'd planned on bringing back to the house. It didn't seem all that pleasant to me now to go all the way to the homeplace again. The agitation inside me was hot enough. Best to let the anger cool by not bringing up bad memories. I turned east and passed through Rattlesnake Gap and stopped at the edge of Andrews Bald in heavy timber on

the south side of Horny Head Mountain. There
I could be well hidden and yet see into the
open area. Six does, a young buck, and one
older buck stood grazing about fifty yards
away, cattycorner to me, just at the edge of the
tree line. They were moving slowly toward me
as they ate. *The bigger buck is what I will take
if I can.* One really good thing Papa had taught
me was to hunt. We needed the meat for food,
and the rest of the deer was put to good use. A
nice tanned hide could make a good warm coat
or a rug to put over Clare or Davie on a cold
winter ride to church.

The meat meant a good roast this week
and jerky for later. Inola's Papa had shown us
how to use the sinew from the muscles to
make string for the bows and arrows we had
played with as children.

I brought him down with one clean shot
into his heart. The others scattered like the
wind. I dressed him out in the edge of the
woods, and it was near total dark when I got
home. Addie had already fed the children.

"I got us a deer today."

"On Sunday?"

I felt bad when she gave me that stare she
did with her head slightly bent and looking at
me out the top of her eyes. Exactly like she did
when she was getting on to the children.

"Yeah. I know it's Sunday, but we got lots
of work to do. I didn't think I would get
another chance. These children need meat to

be strong." She smiled at how I defended my actions.

"Well I can't be too choosy as I am the beggar here. Thank you, Nathe. I had planned to pick some berries tomorrow. That may have to wait a day or two."

I felt better and told her the plan. "I will block out the meat, and you choose what you want to cook now. I'll sharpen my knife again and slice the rest real thin. We can dry it tomorrow. The sun set in a nice red glow, so the weather should be sunny for drying the meat."

"So much for resting on the Sabbath. Let's get to work."

Chapter 12

The sun fanned rays of light that peeked between the leaves on the mountain. It was the makings of a humdinger of a sunset. Darkness would fall like a shade within the next half hour.

The meat was sliced thin, then salted, and herbs rubbed into it. Addie and I had carefully strung the pieces on strings that hung on the porch. She took the knives and pans inside to wash them up. Davie helped me move all the meat to the smokehouse for the night to keep it safe from night time prowling varmints. We would bring it back out to air the next morning.

Addie came tearing out of the house. "Is Clare with you?"

"No, I haven't seen her in a long while." I fastened the smokehouse door.

"Davie, have you seen her?"

"Not in a while. Last time I seen her, she had a bucket and was picking berries out by the road. It looked like she was eating more than she was saving." Davie looked from his mama to me.

Addie picked up the hem of her dress with her left hand and pulled her dress tight to her legs. "I never told her she could pick berries. She's just a baby with no business picking berries by herself. There are snakes all in those berry patches. I will run and see if I can find her."

She ran toward the road and turned down the southern path. "Clare. You come here right this minute. Do you hear me? Answer me, right now. Clare.

I gathered the skin, bones and extra fat from the carcass and sent Davie to take it to the back side of the pasture where the birds and varmints would make quick use of it for their meals.

Addie came back down the road and went in the north direction. "You had better answer me, baby girl. Where are you? Answer me, I said."

I went to the barn. She wasn't in the loft or anywhere around the outside. I peeked in the stall with Maud. Not there. She was not in the tack room.

I heard Addie screaming long before she came in sight. "I can't find her. But I saw her bucket out by the old hog shed above the spring. It was turned over and about a pint of berries was on the ground beside it. She was nowhere to be found. I couldn't pick it up. I left it sitting there. She wouldn't leave her berries like that, would she? Some animal could have gotten her. Anything could have happened to it." Addie started to cry.

"Calm down. I will go and look for her. Is there any place she could have gone? Any other house she might have got in her mind to visit?"

"You know as well as I do that there is not a house for several miles. There is nowhere she could go. Oh no. Please, God, no…She's just a little girl. She can't take care of herself."

"Don't be thinking thoughts like that. We will find her...I will find her. You stay here."

"There's an old pond out behind that hog shed. It has berry bushes all around it. She can't swim. Oh God, she can't swim." Addie wrung her hands and begged me with her eyes to tell her it wasn't what happened.

"Let's not be piling up sorrows before they happen. She is probably fine. I will go and look."

"Hurry, it's starting to get dark. What kind of mother am I? I didn't take care of my baby. She should have been the first thing I took care of. Not food. Not anything else.

I shook her arm roughly. "Stop that. I need you to stop this. Listen for her to yell or watch for her to come back. I can't be worrying about you while I am out looking for her."

"I am sorry. I will look in the places she plays around the house one more time. Please find her. Please."

The bucket was where Addie said. There were a few berries on the ground. The bottom of the bucket was stained purple. It was like she had dropped them from her hands.

Briars tore at my face and hands. One caught in my shirt and tore a rip in the sleeve. I tromped down the bushes all the way around the pond but didn't see her. I watched the mud close over my footprints as I moved my feet. If I had hoped that I would see footprints if she had been here, I was wrong. They would have been gone by now.

The water was muddy. It should have been a little settled if nothing had been in it for a while. Did it mean she had fell into the water, or that maybe a deer or other animal had waded in it recently and drank?

By the time I got back, it was dark. Addie was at the road watching for me. "Did you see anything that made you think something happened to her up there?"

"No. I saw the bucket, but it was not knocked over. She just set it down. I looked around the pond and didn't see anything that made me think she fell in."

Addie started to cry again. "We looked again in the barn and all through the house. We can't find her either."

I put my arm around her. "She will be ok. She'll show up."

"Show up? It's dark. She can't see in the dark. There are bears and wildcats all over these mountains. They will eat her. We have to find her…find her now."

"Let's get some lanterns and I will go out and look."

Hurry…oh please hurry. I am going, too." She wiped the tears with her arm and ran into the house.

"Son, you stay here in case she comes back to the house. Just sit on the porch and listen for her crying.

We went into the kitchen. Addie pulled on the old work boots. I sat down on the floor to fill the lanterns with oil. That's when I saw a hand hanging down from the bench on the far side of the table.

"Addie. Come here. Help me set the table out."

"We ain't got time for that. Hurry with the lamps."

"Just pick up that end and set it out."

There she lay on the bench on her side with her back to the wall.

Addie screamed and grabbed Clare up in her arms. It scared Clare, and she looked wide-eyed at us standing there looking at her. "What's wrong? Why are you all looking at me like that?"

I sat down in a chair in relief and started to laugh. Davie fell in the floor laughing.

"It ain't funny. I was scared tetotally out of my skin." Addie was shaking with relief and anger. She sat Clare on the table and pointed her finger at her. "You scared me to death, baby girl. I thought some animal got you or you drowned in that pond up in the hog pen. What made you come in here and get up on that bench and go to sleep?"

"I was tired of picking berries, and I was sleepy." Her innocent face had a frown on it like that was the strangest question her mama ever asked her.

Addie looked at me and Davie again. She couldn't help but join in our laughter this time, but she sat down on the bench with a sigh of relief. Davie got up and went outside and Clare wondered over to the stove looking for food.

I saw Addie shake and bend at the knees. I thought she would faint.

She raised up when I lay my hand on her back. "I am just glad she's fine. Don't be fussing at her none. We should have watched her better. She only did what was natural for a child to do, go to sleep when she was tired."

Addie nodded her head. "I know. I was just so scared that something bad had happened to my baby girl. I feel weak inside and out. My heart is just a racing and I'm weak.

"Thanks for looking for her."

My neck was stiff and I twisted it to ease the pain. "I was just as concerned as you. I have to admit that when I saw the mud stirred up in that pond, I was too scared to even feel for her body beneath the water. That's horrible, I know, but I just couldn't bring myself to do it. I figured if she had drowned, it was too late, and I did not want to be the one to bring up her body.

"Nathe."

"I'm sorry. It was just how I felt. I was scared too.

"Look at all those scratches on your face. Let me see those hands." Tears pooled in her eyes. "You really did look for her hard." She took a rag and poured water from the dipper on it. "Let me wipe all that blood off your face."

"Ah, that's not needed. I will do it."

"You sit right there and let me wipe your face and hands."

I felt funny inside as she leaned over me and wiped the scratches. I shook as she took each one of my hands in hers and wiped the blood away.

She could feel me trembling. "I better stop this now. Come back in the morning, and

I will put some salve on them. You need strong, well hands for the work we have to do." She turned her back to me, and I left.

Chapter 13

I hitched up the horse to the wagon and brought it to the front of the house. I had tried to dress up. Addie had given me a couple of shirts of Ashe's, and I was wearing one of them with my old breeches.

Clare and Davie sat in the swing that I had made and hung on the front porch. Their Papa had made one before he went to war, but Addie said they had chopped it up and used it for kindling four years ago when Clare had the croup. There was snow on the ground, and they had needed a fire real bad. She had gathered every twig and limb in the yard and out in the field as far as she could and still see the house where Clare lay. Right after that, they moved to her Papa's house for the rest of the winter. They stayed two years there and came back to this house the spring that Clare turned five. Addie said her mama hadn't wanted them to come back, but Addie knew it was time she made a way for her own family. She was a brave woman.

I tried hard to make a difference in the farm in the short time I had been working for them. Part of the fields had been cleared from the young trees that had grown up, and the barn and tack were now in good shape. The land was ready for corn to be planted.

I watched the front porch, waiting for Addie to come out. On a rainy day last week, I had made the swing from lumber I bought down from the trip to East Laporte.. Addie was happy as a lark. She brought out two straight chairs and made it look like a real friendly front porch.

"Davie Tom and Clare, get on in the wagon now. Yore mama will be ready to go in a minute."

Davie crawled into the wagon and looked at me. "Are you going with us to church?"

I thought I might as well go. I need to make sure the wheel I fixed doesn't come off. You never know about other people's workmanship. I want you all to be safe." That lie tasted bitter in my mouth. I knew that Inola would be conscientious in his work. But one excuse was as good as another if you had to have one.

Addie came out of the house with her purse. She stopped and put a handkerchief inside it. I ran to the edge of the porch and took her hand. She looked surprised that I was dressed for church but smiled at me and let me help her down the steps.

"Thank you Nathe. But I have been going up and down these steps by myself for a number of years without help."

My face turned red. "I know ma'am but, with you all dressed up like that and with that dress standing out with some kind of petticoat under there, I wasn't sure you could see your feet...."

Addie cut her eyes over to me as I took her elbow. "I can see my feet just fine, Nathe Milsaps."

"That really is a mighty pretty dress, Miss Addie. I mean all your dresses are pretty, but I have never seen this one."

"I only have two Sunday dresses, Nathe. Surely you have seen me wear this one." She took her hand and slid it down her dress and looked down. "Mama made the dress for me before I moved back here to the farm. I love it." She smiled at me. "Thank you for noticin, though."

"You're welcome."

As I helped her into the wagon, Davie piped out. "Just like a real family. A mama and a Papa. Us two kids. All going to church together. Ain't it nice, Mama?"

"David Thomas Fisher, you just hush your mouth."

"But Mama, Nathe would make a fine husband for you. He respects you. He calls you ma'am and does all kind of things to please you, compliments your cooking and yore pretty dress. He would make a fine Papa. He whittled me a whistle and fixed a corn shuck doll for Clare. So he cares about us children too."

Addie looked horrified and had a coughing fit.

"You said you didn't want no man from these parts that you have ever seen. All the available ones just want to drink and feud, and you had had about as much of that as you can stand. But Nathe ain't from around here. He's from Tennessee."

Addie had another coughing spell and, when she raised her head, tears were in her eyes. I didn't know if she was laughing or crying. "Davie sit down in the back of the wagon, and shut yore mouth."

"But, Mama…"

"Not another word, Davie."

Davie was not known for being quiet. He didn't say a word to his mama, but I heard him tell Clare, "Next week, I'm going to see Grandma. She'll know something I can do to make sure Nathe and Mama like each other enough to get married. There is nothing she don't know. When we lived with her, she told me that if I sang before breakfast, I would cry before dinner. It happened every time. One time I was standing there with my hands locked behind my head. Grandma knocked my hands down and she said, 'It's bad luck to do that. To lock your hands behind your head means yore mama will die.' It scared me about half to death. Grandpa said, 'Or it could mean you just got arrested by the sheriff.' Grandma threw a dishrag at him. I figured it will be worth a try to find out what saying or potion she has to win a man for Mama."

I reached up and used my hands to pinch my lips. I didn't think she would appreciate it if I laughed. Addie looked straight ahead and pretended she didn't hear a word Davie said.

xxx

Two other wagons got to the church at the same time as we did. Four others had already tied up their horses, and the people were inside the house of worship. Once inside, I realized that one was Inola and Synthee. She was holding a tiny baby, and the women had gathered around her to see it. Addie took her turn, and then came back to sit beside me.

"It's a boy, Nathe. Ain't he just as pretty as a peach?"

"Boys ain't pretty Addie. They're handsome."

She waved her hand at me. "Pshaw, boys his age can be pretty. It's been so long since I had a baby at my house. Both my babies were pretty. Davie Tom looked just like me, Ashe said. Of course he never got to see Clare. But she looked just like Davie did as a baby."

I reached over and whispered low enough no one could hear. "Well no wonder they were pretty then…if they looked just like you."

Oh my. Addie blushed from the hairline on her forehead to the bottom of her neck where it slipped into her dress. "You hush now, Nathe. You're just saying that. You don't mean it."

"You will find I don't say things I don't mean."

She smiled and looked back toward Synthee and the baby.

Inola looked at me and nodded slightly. It seemed strange to see him in church. He sat stiffly beside his wife and talked very little to anyone. He did not look Indian at all except that he was slightly darker than the other men. Not that I felt anyone cared. Indians had been a part of our lives for as long as I had been alive. And probably everyone else here. They were just people.

After church, the women went back to admiring Synthee and Inola's baby boy right outside the church door. I walked over to Inola's wagon and shook his hand.

"Never saw you at a church before. Did you go when you were a boy?"

"My father was an Adawehi, a mythkeeper, for the Cherokee and it would not have been right. His father also was an Adawehi. My grandfather hid in the mountains when the others were forced to leave. So did about a thousand others. Grandfather was twenty years old in 1838, and my Papa was a small boy at the time. When I was a child, living nearby the river and playing in these woods with you, my papa thought it was time to come out and live a normal life. But to remain outside the land where they said we were to live. But we would visit family and father would tell them the great myths. It hurt my mother that her family was forced to move away. They died on the journey. At that time, my mother took the white man's religion, but papa never would. It made my mother sad. I should be an Adawehi as well, but I cannot do that to my wife. It makes Synthee happy for me to be here. So I am happy, too."

"So that is why your father told us so many old stories of the Cherokee. I thought he was just a good storyteller."

Inola smiled and nodded. "He was a good storyteller. I miss him."

"He's gone?"

"Yes for six years now. It was a hunting accident they said. He was accidently shot when he was going back to see his brothers on the reservation. But I know many were angry that he refused to live there like the others did. Both white men and our own Cherokee men were not happy with his decision. 'An Adawehi should live with his people.' The tribe said. 'He's an Indian and should live with his people.' The white man said. Perhaps it was just a hunting accident. I don't know. My mother was old and ill. That is why I went back to the reservation."

Addie was shooing the children into the wagon. "I will remember to call you John. You must call me Nathe Milsaps."

He shook his head in agreement. "I will do it my friend. But secrets make life very difficult, don't they? Hopefully there will come a day when secrets will not be necessary.

Inola put his hand on my shoulder. "I am unsure I should tell you what I am about to say..."

"You can tell me anything, my friend." Inola's face looked so serious. I tried to reassure him.

He shook his head no. "I know that I can, but should I? When I know it could bring harm to another or perhaps even to you? It is only because I promised you that I will do it. It is about one of the Hooper men that killed your family. But before I tell you, you must also promise me something."

"What is that?" I did not like to break promises and wanted to make them sparingly.

"That you will think long and hard before you do anything about what I tell you. That you will count the cost of your actions. Many men have not done so, and found that the price was higher than they had really wanted to pay. If you act on this, it may change the path that you are now on and the outcome will be at odds with what I think you really want."

"You think you are surer of what I want than me? I have had many years to think about it. There is nothing I am surer about than what I want to do to those men. An eye for an eye and tooth for a tooth. Life for a life."

"I ask you again to think about it. Find a way to get past your hurt. The rambling dreams of an orphaned boy should not make the decision for a grown man, in the position you are now in. Rethink it, Nathe. Lay out your paths as a grown man and see if this act will put you on a path that will carry you away from the dreams of a man. I tell you, a little boy should not make those kind of decisions."

"You are going to tell me about one of the Hoopers, am I right? What is his name?"

"It is Levi Hooper."

xxx

That afternoon we ate the beans that Addie had soaked the night before, placed on the stove while she fixed breakfast, and left to cook while we were gone. The house was hot, so we ate on the porch.

I watched the children play. I took a knife and went across the road and cut a young sapling and brought it to the porch. Addie sat in the swing, and I sat on the step. She watched Clare, and I whittled and notched the wood. I took the sinew I had dried from the deer and tied it to one end of the three foot section of the sapling. It bent easily, and I tied the other end to make a bow. The shorter sections I used to make arrows.

Davie came running to my side. He had found feathers in the chicken house and brought them to me. On each arrow, I notched a section of the bark and slipped in the feathers and bound them with more dried sinew. Then I made a "v" in the end of the arrow to place the string of the bow. Inola had shown me how to make arrows and bows many years ago.

After I gave him instructions on using the bow and arrows, Davie shot into the trees at make believe squirrels and shot into the grass around the barn at rabbits. I went back to the porch.

Addie pushed her feet against the floor and backed up the swing as far as she could and then let her legs go. Her girlish squeal as it went higher and higher made my chest feel strange. She was like a young, carefree girl, for a moment without a worry in the world.

She slid her feet against the boards and brought the swing back to a gentle back and forth movement and began to sing.

> "Wanted— a hand to hold my own,
>   As down life's vale I glide;
>   Wanted— an arm to lean upon,
>   Forever by my side.
>   Wanted— a firm and steady foot,

With step secure and free,
To take its straight and onward
pace,
Over life's path with me.

Wanted— a hand to hold my own,
As down life's vale I glide;
Wanted— an arm to lean upon,
Forever by my side.

Wanted— a form erect and high,
A head above my own;
So much that I might walk
beneath
Its shadow o'er me thrown.
Wanted— an eye, within whose
depth
Mine own might look, and see
Uprisings from a guileless
heart,
O'erflown with love for me.

Wanted— a lip, whose kindest smile
Would speak for me alone;
A voice, whose richest melody
Would breathe affection's tone.
Wanted— a true, religious soul,
To pious purpose given,
With whom my own might pass
along
The road that leads to Heaven.

Wanted— a hand to hold my own,
As down life's vale I glide;
Wanted— an arm to lean upon,
Forever by my side." (1)

Her voice had the sweetness of an angel.

".....Forever—by—my—side." She
repeated.

I caught her eye and, we stared at each
other. She smiled gently and bowed her head.

"What are you going to make me, Nathe?"
The tiny, soft voice of Clare could melt an
icicle in the dead of winter, and her face was a
looking glass image of Addie. Her mama must
have been a beautiful child.

"What if we play a game instead?"

She came and stood in front of me. "What
game?"

"Well, how about hide and seek?"

She shook her head up and down in
excitement.

"Davie you want to play? That bow and
arrow will still be here later."

"Ok. You count, and we will hide."

I hid my eyes. "One, two, three, four, five,
six…" I counted to one hundred. "Bushel of
wheat, bushel of rye, all not hid, holler I."

Not one sound came.

"Bushel of wheat, bushel of clover. All
not hid, can't hide over. All eyes open. Here I
come."

Two little dirty feet stuck out just below
me on the steps, but I pretended not to see.

"Addie, have you seen two children
around here…one boy about yea high and the
cutest little girl that anyone ever laid eyes on?"
Clare giggled.

"There she is. Let me see if I can pull her out of there." I reached down and pulled on her toes. Davie came running when he thought I was not looking.

"Home free." It was the second time I had seen Davie act like the child he was. It was a wonderful thing.

"You both are just too good at this game. I guess I will have to try again."

Several times of that, and we were all worn out.

Addie stopped singing, swung gently, and watched us play. I sat down beside her.

"Thank ye, Nathe. Those younguns haven't had that much fun in ages and ages."

The wind had gotten up, and clouds gathered over the mountain. A storm was coming.

Addie leaned forward. "Davie, get old Maude into the barn."

"I can do that." I placed my hand on her arm.

Addie looked at my hand and then at my face. "No, it won't hurt him none to put up the horse. You can sit a spell here if you like." She motioned to Davie to go on. "Clare, get your doll, and take it on into the house. There's a pan of water in there. Wash your feet and ready yourself for bed."

Davie got the horse up and shut the doors to the barn. The rain was starting to beat down in large drops as he stepped on the porch.

I went into the yard and picked up a stick that was charred on one end from a fire that Addie had kindled to heat the pot for washing clothes. "Come here you two. I want to draw around your feet and leave their mark here on the porch."

Clare laughed and wiggled her feet. "That tickles. No…oh my feet are so ticklish."

"Come on Davie, let me do yours right beside hers."

The charred stick drew the exact size of their feet side by side. This would come in handy for me to make the soles for the shoes I wanted to make them before winter set in.

"Wash yore feet, girl, before you get in that bed, and wash 'em good. Go wash your feet Davie, and go on up to bed, too. I will be in shortly to tuck you both in."

Clomp, drag, clomp. Clare came to the door with one of her mama's Sunday shoes on. "Mama someday I can wear your shoes?"

"Little girl, get that shoe off. Don't you know it's bad luck to walk in just one shoe. What am I going to do with you? You will bring bad luck on the whole house."

"Aw Addie, surely there ain't no such thing as bad luck. You're like my mama used to be. Just superstitious. All kinds of wives tales and sayings."

"Hmph…you think not. You just wait and see if it ain't bad luck. Something will happen you just wait and see. I imagine if you think about it, your mama was always right too. Just admit it."

We sat quietly swinging back and forth, watching the storm move from mountain to mountain, storm after storm descending on us.

"I love rain, Nathe. Never have figured out why, unless it's because when it rains all our hard work stops and for a little while we can rest. And, the fact that it is so fresh smelling. It just washes the world clean. Seems like everything in these mountains is dirty most of the time. Dusty and gritty with dirt. Rain carries it all away. "

If I spoke, it might break the spell between us, so I kept quiet.

"The rain also makes me feel safe."

I couldn't help myself. I had to ask. "Safe? What kind of things do you fear?"

She blushed. "Well, I don't have time to be afraid of much of anything anymore but, when I was a child, I was always askeered that someone was going to come into our house and chop off our heads or maybe take Mama and Papa."

I shivered. *Chop off their heads?* The words brought back painful thoughts. I understood her thinking. The same feelings had been with me for ages after I went to Tennessee.

"And my childish thinking was that nobody in their right mind would be out in the rain, so I felt safe." She smiled and showed a deep dimple in each cheek. "You think I am silly don't you, Nathe?"

"No I don't think you are silly. I think you are like every other child with common childish fears and reasoning."

"I feel safe now."

"But it's not raining anymore." I reached out and touched her hair.

"I know. But I still feel safe. It might be because you are here. You make me feel safe."

"Addie…"

"Mama, are you coming to tuck me in." Clare sounded like she was going to cry.

"Coming, baby girl. I will be right there."

She walked to the back door, then looked back at me. "You might oughtta be back in the barn when I get her tucked in, Nathe Millsaps."

I bit my lip but smiled in spite of myself. "Yeah, that might be a good idea." The swing creaked as I stood up.

Addie opened the door a smite but looked back one more time. "We did feel like a family for a little bit like Davie said, didn't we?"

I nodded in agreement.

Chapter 14

There was no smoke coming from the chimney when I came out of the barn the next morning. Something was bad wrong. Every day since I arrived at Addie's, she had a cooked breakfast of some sorts waiting for me and the children. My foot caught on the porch, and I fell on the steps. Addie opened the door. She threw water from a pan into the yard and picked up a bucket and poured the last fresh water into the empty pan.

"Take this bucket up to the spring, and get cold water. Clare has been sick since right after I tucked her in. She started out vomiting, and now she has the trots. Her fever is really high. Since the wee hours of the morning I've been putting wet rags on her head to cool her."

"What caused her to be sick?"

"I don't know, and I have no idea what else to do right now. I can't think clear." Addie pushed back her hair with her arm and started to cry. "She will scarcely eat or drink anything."

I wanted to go to her and tell her everything was going to be alright. As soon as my foot set down on the porch she shouted, "Just get some cold water. Hurry."

There was another bucket at the spring, and I filled them both. It might be good to boil a potato and try to get her to drink it. The only medicine I could remember, other than roots and leaves, were some that Jonathan's aunt from the North had brought to us the first winter I was in Tennessee during the war. She had sewn it into her petticoat to get by the Union soldiers that checked the baggage of anyone coming south in case they were smuggling in supplies for the Confederates. And, of course, I didn't know what medicine it was or where to get it now.

I brought the water inside the house and took the rags and rinsed them in cold water and gave them back to Addie. The potatoes were the ones I had graveled from the end of the row in the potato patch. I sliced them thin and put in water. The potatoes boiled down to a thick soup. I added salt and some meat grease.

"Let me try to feed her."

I sat on the edge of the bed near Clare. Her skin was pale, and her eyes remained closed. I slipped a tiny spoonful between her lips, and she swallowed at my bidding, still not opening her eyes. Addie nodded her head and was pleased when Clare had eaten a teacup full.

I took the cup to the table and put it in the wash pan. I heard gagging behind me. Clare puked on the bed. I slipped my arms under her and raised her hot body off the bed. She looked at me sadly. She was pitiful.

Addie pulled the quilt off and put down a clean one. Clare's eyes closed, and she fell back to sleep.

Addie laid down beside her and closed her eyes.

Davie followed me to the barn. "She shore is sick. Do you think she will be ok?"

"I hope so. Children get sick easy but get over it really fast, I reckon. Never was around little children much. I didn't have brothers and sisters in Tennessee."

My mind was occupied fixing the leather harness and replaced missing boards on the corncrib, but I stayed close to the house in case Addie needed me. She came out once and asked for white oat bark, which was easy enough to come by. There was a tree by the barn.

She shook her head as she went back to the house, saying something about *one shoe on and one shoe off...bad luck.*

We ate leftover beans and cornbread for dinner and supper that day.

xxx

At breakfast the next morning, Clare was still sick. She laid in her mama's bed, her face pale with bright red spots on each cheek.

Addie put out a plate for me and Davie, and piled on eggs that she had fried. She took out biscuits from the oven.

I walked over to the bed and touched Clare's forehead. "She's still hot Addie. Hotter than I ever felt on a person." Clare's eyes fluttered open. She looked at me, and tears dripped on the bed. It was like she was begging me to help. Crying was the only way she could say it.

Addie sat down on the edge of the bed and looked weary. "She's been that way all night. I didn't sleep much. She slept fitfully. I kept a cool rag on her forehead most all night. I thought she would be better by now.

"I tried that white oak bark made into a tea during the night, but it hain't helped at all. I really need you to go and get me some roots for her. She's growing weaker. And, as we don't have some fine southern lady that can bring in some high falutin medicine in the hem of her petticoat like you told Davie, I want you to go over to the base of Otter Mountain, down by Pistol creek, and find me some Yellowroot. Make sure you find a place with at least three plants and take only one. There has to be some left to make more plants. Mama sent me there one time to get some for Clarece, my sister, when she had the bloody flux. It's the best this mountain has to give for such."

"I wouldn't know yellow root from anything but sing-sang. That is about all I ever gathered for my mama. She collected them herself and dried the plants and roots, and then put them in jars for when she'd need them."

Addie wrung her hands. "Don't you make me feel bad for not doing that. I guess I didn't expect my family to get sick. Not this sick for sure. They never have ailed much in their lives. They've always been strong and healthy. A good mother would plan for things like this and be prepared." Tears gathered in her eyes, and I felt as low as a snake's belly.

"Ah, I'm sorry. You just tell me what to get, and I'll do my best to get it and bring it on back here. Surely there are some roots nearer to the house we could use."

"That's the only place I know that they grow. There may be some but we can't afford to be searching. Go where I know they are, and get them."

"Tell me what to get. Whatever you say."

Addie described the plant whiles I ate breakfast. "Yellowroot likes the mountainside, down close by a stream. It grows up about a foot or two with a stalk that shoots out with a cluster of thin leaves about six inches long. There are about five leaves to a cluster, and they have jagged teeth along the edge of the leaf. By now, they may have purple looking or brown flowers, sometimes just one bloom, sometimes a bunch of blooms. When you pull it up, its roots will be long and yellow. If you pinch a bit off and put it on your tongue, it will be bitter. It's the roots that I use. While you are there, go ahead and get some sing-sang, so I can build up her blood, too."

The 'sang" won't be no problem. I just hope I can find the right thing for yellowroot."

"You got to find it. And real soon. She's bad, real bad. I should have already been doctoring her earlier than I have. Just kept hoping she'd get better on her own. I was foolish."

Addie stood and began to stack our plates to take to the sink. Instead she sat back down with her eyebrows pulled tight together. "If you can't find that, get some sweet fern. That might work too."

My face showed my ignorance. Addie let out a deep breath. "Well, let me tell you about it, too.

"Sweet fern can be found down by the lower part of the stream before you go up Otter Mountain. There where the Mills family has cleared that woodland or down by the side of the water where there is gravel and rocks. It's weedy looking and smells sweet. Its branches are slim and reddish-brown. It may be chest tall on you but, down there, most likely will be shorter. The stem has a whole bunch of leaves that are hairy like and kind of rounded with some teeth. You won't have to worry about counting the plants as there are probably a bunch of them together. Deer like to eat it. Get me the whole plant. I can put two spoons of fresh leaves of that into boiling water and make some tea. It's good for flux, also. My mama told me so.

"Hurry up and leave, so as you can get back as fast as you can. She can't keep nothing down as to what just comes right back up, or out her bottom side. The sun is already overhead. If you ride by moonlight tonight, it will still be about daybreak before you get back. I wish I knew where some was closer to tell you about, but I don't. That's not far from Papa's and where Mama gets it. Hurry."

I saddled up Maude. Addie came out with a work shirt of Ashe's and some string. She had tied string around the cuffs of the long-sleeved shirt. "Put the plants in these here shirt sleeves so you won't lose them."

"Yes ma'am. I'll be back as soon as I can."

"Make it sooner than later,. I'm afeered she will not last long without the medicines. If you want her to live as much as me, you'd better git on down there and get back. I don't know what I'd do if…"

Chapter 15

The moon had faded with the light of the sun that rose over the mountains to the east. Maude was in a sweat, and so was I. Addie was sitting in the swing on the porch.

"I got the herbs you told me to get. I brought back the top as well as the root, so you could check and make sure it was the right root."

Her eyes stared far away into the woods. She didn't answer me. Her legs stopped the swing, and she bent over and placed her head in her hands.

"Addie. Addie look here at me. I got the roots to make her well."

"Too late, Nathe. Too late." She raised up and stared out into the early light of the morning and rocked her body back and forth. She sang the same lullaby she'd been singing to Clare for the past two days.

Oh God. Please no…Please, I beg you. The house was deathly quiet except for the squeak of the door when I opened it. There she lay on the bed, her eyes slightly open, and a gentle smile on her lips. The corn shuck doll I'd made was clutched in her hand.

I couldn't tell if it was me or Addie screaming until I choked out the words. "Nooooo…It's not true." I picked up her limp body and placed my face again her cold one. "I got you herbs, baby girl. It will be ok. You'll be ok." The doll fell from her limp hand onto the bed.

I felt Addie's hand on my back, and I turned. "She's done gone. I thought she'd get well." The bed creaked with my weight when I sat down on it with her still in my arms. Addie sat down beside me. "My baby girl has done gone on to heaven. I didn't think she was sick unto death."

Tears streamed down her face, and she reached and picked up Clare's tiny fingers with her right hand and placed them on the palm of her own left hand. She patted and kissed it and then took both of Clare's hands and put them to her face. "Tell your daddy I

did the best I could to keep you safe. He made
me promise in my last letters to him that I
would keep you safe from harm. Let him know
you didn't die because of no feuding or
fighting. Tell him I did all that I knew to do for
ye." She pulled Clare's body from my arms
and took her to the porch and began to swing.

Sleep my baby on my bosom
Warm and cozy will it prove
Round thee mother's arms are folding
In her heart a mother's love

There shall no one come to harm thee
Naught shall ever break thy rest
Sleep my darling babe in quiet
Sleep on mother's gentle breast.

Sleep serenely, baby, slumber
Lovely baby, gently sleep;
Tell me wherefore art thou smiling
Smiling sweetly in thy sleep?

Do the angels smile in heaven
When thy happy smile they see?
Dost thou on them smile while slumb'ring
On my bosom peacefully.

Do not fear the sound of a breeze
Brushing leaves against the door.
Do not dread the murmuring seas,
Lonely waves washing the shore.

Sleep child mine, there's nothing here,
While in slumber at my breast,
Angels smiling, have no fear,
Holy angels guard your rest. (2)

I pulled a chair beyond the reach of Addie's feet as she swung. She kept singing the song over and over.

The footprints that I drew with the charred stick in front of the swing would be a reminder for many a day. I never would get to make her those shoes to wear. Those tiny feet had walked in snow and got more splinters and stubbed toes than I wanted to think about. To die and never know the feeling of a good pair of shoes that protected your feet. It just wasn't right. Why had I put off making those shoes? Her mama would never see her marry nor have her own children. I needed to hold her one more time.

"Let me take her, Addie. I'll hold her for a little bit." She stared at me and smiled the saddest smile I had ever seen on a human. She stood up and swung her from side to side like you were soothing a baby that was a-crying.

"She loved you Nathe. She played with that doll every day since you made it. She fixed tea and made mud pies with those little acorn shells, after you showed her how. I always knew she would make a good mama. She always made sure that doll had a good bed and wrapped her up if she thought it was cold. She sang her sweet songs. She knew every

word of the song I just sang to her. Early
yesterday, she asked me to make sure
"Frances" didn't get what she had. She didn't
want her sick. Those were the last words she
ever spoke that I could understand."

Addie handed Clare to me and sat back
down in the swing and watched me rock her.

"She died in the early morning hours. I
was asleep and woke to her taking her last
breath." She looked at Clare in my arms and
then out to the barn. But I felt she was looking
more into the future than
 anywhere here. "Yep, she would have been a
good mama. But that was not meant to be, it
seems. She has done gone on to heaven to be
with Ashe. She was but only a baby when he
died in the war. He never even got to see her.
Do you think she'll know he's her daddy, or
him know her, Nathe?"

"Of course they'll know each other. He's
probably been watching all this and waiting
for her to come to him, once he knew she was
sick unto death."

"Do you think?"

"From what you tell me, he was a good
Papa. I believe he'll know her. She's probably
already in his arms now. Just a hugging him,
like she did me when I came in from the
fields…." My heart felt like it was going to
bust into tiny little pieces. I don't think I could
have loved her more if she was my own flesh
and blood. She was so loving and kind. Her
little brown eyes always smiled long before

her mouth did. They'd light up when I came in, and soon she'd be jumping and dancing, begging me to sit by her at supper.

Addie got up but didn't look at me. "The Lord gives and the Lord takes away. There's nothing else I can do. A piece of me just died along with her. I don't think I'll ever be whole again. I want you to take her into the house, and lay her on the bed. The last thing I can do for her is to bathe her real good and dress her up in that little flowerdy dress she loved to wear to church. We'll bury her in that. Mama would want me to find a white dress, but she loved this one the best. But I don't have a white dress and no time or money to make one.

"You take Davie, and go and tell the preacher. He seems to have a way of letting others know about things like this. Mama and Papa have gone to my sister's house in Asheville and won't be back for at least five more days. They couldn't make it back for the funeral even if they knew about it."

"Where's Davie?"

"Probably out in the barn. He was with me when she died. I woke and sat up straight in bed. I must have heard something. Davie was laying at my feet, and he raised up. Clare looked over at him and then over his shoulder toward the door. She took a deep breath, looked back at me, gazed into my eyes, and smiled the prettiest little smile you ever seed. I thought she was coming out of it, but then she let out air and never took in another breath. I knew she was gone. I looked at Davie, and he knew by my face she'd died. He stared at her, then took off in the direction of the barn. Leave him be for a little longer. He'll come in when he's ready. You and him can go to the church then."

Addie pulled back the covers on her bed, and I lay Clare on the sheet.

"Stoke the fire Nathe. I will get water from the back porch, and we'll heat it for her bath."

Addie washed her face and then got fresh warm water on the cloth for her hands, wetting and wringing it out after every little section of her body. "She's so cold. Get me a blanket. Do you think the water is warm enough?"

I got a blanket and tucked it around her body and helped Addie pull back a little piece at a time until she finished washing and then dressed her. She covered her back up with the blanket to her chin.

"She was born right here on this bed. This very bed. She was even conceived right here. Now she stays her last night right on it. Don't you think it's strange that we live and die in the same place. Never going nowhere." She looked at me. "I guess you don't think about it like that as you lived in Tennessee, outside these mountains. These mountains are new to you."

I went to the porch and threw the pan of water out into the yard. Addie followed me.

"Will you fare well enough while I am gone to tell the preacher? I hate to leave you alone."

Addie smiled. "I will be glad to have a little time along with my baby girl before she is put in the cold ground. It will be all the time I have to…." She swallowed hard.

Davie walked out from the barn and up to the porch.

Addie continued. "I'll be fine. I will change the sheets and get her all laid out for company."

"As soon as Davie and I get back, I'll take the lumber I had for that gate I was going to make and use it for her coffin, if that'll do." Davie opened the door and stared at Clare on the bed.

"Thank you for making her a good box, Nathe. That lumber will be fine. Tell the preacher we will bury her by my grandmother in the church graveyard. See if he can get someone to dig us a grave for her. Davie, go with Nathe to get the preacher."

Davie closed the door and waited for me to bring the wagon up to the house.

xxx

We were almost to the pastor's house before Davie said a word.

"It's my fault. I was sick a week ago with the same thing. She done caught it from me."

"Twasn't your fault. Not anyone's fault. Things like this happen. No one knows why. You got better, but for some unknownst reason she didn't."

"She couldn't eat nor drink for the past two days except for that tater soup you made. And she puked that back up. She was so pale, and anything we tried to make her drink came right back up. I was like that at first too, but after one day I was a better. Why didn't she get better?"

"I haven't any idee. Some people are just weaker and can't fight the sickness I guess. A person can't live long without drinking, that's for sure. But don't you go blaming yourself. It doesn't do anybody any good if we start blaming. It could be me for not getting back quick enough with the roots, or not leaving sooner to go and get them. I was just skeered I would get the wrong thing and make her sicker. I should have gone on and tried, but I waited too long. You see, any of us could take some blame. But that won't bring her back. We just have to know she's with your Papa now and is not sick anymore. It's like the pastor preached last week from the Bible. David's boy died and he said 'I can't bring him back, but I can go to him'. That will have to be the way we leave it."

Davie seemed to think about all I had said and didn't mention it the rest of the way home.

The preacher was in the church when we went by. I opened the door and stepped inside.

I told him what happened and he seemed to know just how to handle things.

"I guess we need to have that funeral tomorrow afternoon. Not good to wait much longer as the days are pretty warm and the body will begin to show the wear from it. Too bad Addie's mama and papa won't get back. She is really going to need them. It's a good thing you are there, Nathe. She will have you to watch out for them until she can take this all in and try to move on with life without Clare. She was such a sweet child. Hard to believe she won't be here at church no more."

I nodded. "Thanks for everything, just in case I forget to tell you later."

xxx

Late that afternoon, people brought in food. They put it on the table or the cook stove. Then they went by the bed and looked at Clare and shook their heads.

I made the box and brought it in.

Addie walked with me to the bed to help move her to the coffin. "Davie, go upstairs and get Clare's quilt off her bed."

I picked Clare up. Addie carefully folded the quilt and placed it where the middle portion would lay beneath Clare's body and the lower part would partially cover her. She rolled the upper end of the quilt under and made it a pillow for her head. The pastor held the pillow in place.

Addie moved to the side and said. "Tomorrow, just make sure you pull this out and place it over her head before you close her up." She walked over to the table while the pastor and I got her into the box and straightened the quilt.

I put the box toward the middle of the bed, tucked covers underneath it, and raised it up just a little. I felt a gentle crunch under my foot and leaned over and pulled the cornshuck doll out from under the edge of the bed. I placed it by Clare's hand and pulled the quilt over the body of the doll.

Addie came to my side. "That looks real nice. She would have liked you covering it up like that." Tears ran down my face, and I wiped then with the back of my hand. Addie reached up and patted me on the shoulder.

The pastor told us the grave had been dug and was ready for the funeral tomorrow. "Do you want the words said here or down at the church?"

Addie didn't take her eyes off Clare's face. "Clare loved to go to church, and I want her to be able to be there one more time. So if it makes no difference to you, we'll just have the service there. Me and Nathe and Davie will bring her by wagon tomorrow morning. And a couple of men can tote her up the hill after the service to the grave site. She's just a tiny little thing and don't weigh much."

He nodded and left.

Addie had not eaten since Clare died, but with a little encouragement from church women setting up the table and washing up dishes as people ate, she did get to the table and picked up a plate.

The preacher's wife reached around Addie and set a plate on the table and said aloud, "I hope you don't mind. I saw these looked ripe as we passed your garden, and I picked one and cut it up."

I heard the plate hit the floor, and Addie covered her face with her hands and screamed "No, no, no."

I ran to her side and saw the wedges of watermelon. As plain as day, I heard the words she said the day we were planting. I was sure she remembered them just as clearly. 'I can't wait till these watermelons are ripe, and we can eat them.'

Addie went back to the bed and sat by Clare.

I grabbed the platter and went to the back door and flung the watermelon as far as I could throw it.

The preacher's wife stooped and picked up Addie's broken plate. She whimpered and swiped at her eyes with her upper arm. I bent to one knee behind her and helped. I whispered mine and Addie's conversation that we had had that day in the garden.

"Oh, Nathe. I am so sorry. I wish I had known."

"There's no way you could have. She's not mad at you. Don't feel bad. It would have happened anyway. If not this day, then another. Everything will make its rounds in her head. Almost everything she ever said to Clare, good and bad. Those times she had to punish her. When she was sick. Things that she feels like hastened the day. Don't be upset with her, ma'am. She'll be alright."

"Thank ye Nathe. Will you apologize for me when she feels a little better? I don't think I would be able to mention this to her. I am sick about it."

"Surely I will."

Several church people sat up all night with her body. I tried to get Addie to go up to the loft and lay down but she wouldn't. "I can sleep when I can't be with her no more. I will be right here by her side as long as I can."

I could understand that, and I didn't ask her again.

Chapter 16

The service was one that Clare would have liked. They sung more songs than I had heard at a funeral, but that was the part that she'd have loved.

I took one end of the coffin, and one of the elders of the church took the other. Preacher Marshall led the way, us behind with the body, then Addie with Davie's hand in hers. Friends and neighbors followed. I stood to the side and looked around at the graveyard as the pastor prayed a beautiful prayer. Leaning against a tree on the edge of the grounds stood Amps. He nodded at me, and I quickly bowed my head. It embarrassed me that I had been looking around. When I looked up, Amps was gone and I never saw him again during the rest of the burial.

Inola was there as well. He stayed after many others left. We stood together and watched as Addie sat by the grave and wept.

"Life is not easy my friend. For any of us. Especially for you and your friend today. No one should have to outlive their children. There is something very wrong with that. Yet it happens many times."

"Clare was a special child."

"I know. I saw you with her many times at church. She could not have loved you more had you been her father, Nathe."

It was hard to swallow the need to throw myself on her grave and beg God to let her come back.

If anyone knew about grief, it was Inola. "You have seen much sadness, Inola. I know."

"The Cherokee have seen much sorrow. It is the way of life for everyone here it seems. The movement of my family to the west. Many dying along the way, or separated from family and never to see them again. I heard stories of how families that were sitting down to eat, and the soldiers would come in and drive them from their home and land. Men sometimes were working in the fields, and they were drug to their houses and gathered with their wives and children and forced to move…the last thing they saw was their house in flames."

I knew there were many with pain, as bad if not worse than mine, but it did not make me feel any better. "At least many were together as a family. Their fathers were not killed like mine, or their children taken from them."

"That was true for some, but do you think it was easier for them to watch as the cold and sickness took their children along the way?"

"No, I am sure it was not."

"My friend, it may not be the time to speak of this, but you have come back for some reason that I feel is going to cause much more heartache than satisfaction. Don't do what you are feeling. Let go of the need to even things. Let it go."

There were too many things weighing on me. Too much pain. Too much sorrow. My mind could not think.

It was hard to get Addie to leave the graveyard.

"I am hungry, mama." Davie pulled at his mama's arm.

"None of us have eaten today Addie. Let's take the boy home, and fix some supper."

She nodded and looked one last time at the grave and turned and walked to the wagon. I had tied the horse to a tree by the church.

The pastor was standing in the doorway looking up on the mountain. "Nathe, ain't that smoke yonder coming from about where Addie's place is."

I felt a dread come over me and looked to where he was pointing. "Yes, that does look

about where we live. We better hurry on and
see what is going on."

xxx

Addie looked worried. "Hurry Nathe. That
smoke cloud is getting bigger and bigger. Do
you think the house is burning?"

"I don't think so. We didn't leave a lamp
on anywhere. There ain't been no lightning or
anything today. There was no cooking done
and no fire in the fireplace. Why would the
house catch on fire?"

We were still about a mile away when we
realized it was the house or barn, or maybe
both. Davie was crying. My eyes burned, and
I was angry. *What would cause either one to
burn today? There was no reason for it. No
lightning. No lamps. Nothing. Not unless
someone set it on fire. But why would anyone
do that?*

It was the house. It was too far gone to
even try to fight it. Everything Addie owned
was gone. Some neighbor men, and even a few
families, were at the house by the time it all
ended. Each one shaking their head and
wondering how it could have happened.

By dark, the only ones left were Preacher
Marshall and a man that lived nearby the
church, Jed Dooley. The preacher sat with
Addie and tried to comfort her. Meanwhile Jed
and I took a broom and swept out the empty
corn crib. I brought the cornshuck mattress

from my place in the barn and placed it on a frame I had made from boards pulled from the chicken house. It would do for the night for Addie and Davie. There were promises of some pieces of furniture from people at the church to come on the morrow. Addie stood looking at the smoldering logs. I laid my hand on her arm. She didn't look up. "That's the second house in this very spot that has burned to the ground. If I build again, it has to sit farther back. Not on the same spot."

"It's not the land that caused the fire."

"I know that. But is sure seems unlucky. Mama told me not to build here. She said it would come to no good end. Why didn't I listen?"

I folded my arms and stood beside her, both watching smoke roll into the sky from a puff of wind. "I know your family have all these sayings and fool reasoning, but it was somebody that did this. Not where the house sat."

"You know nothing about my family. Nothing a-tall. Don't judge us. We have reasons for our sayings, and they have served us well. They came with our family when they settled in this country, and there is no good reason to let them go now."

She walked away from me. I hoped it was because of the smoke that blew toward us with the changing wind direction.

I settled Addie into the corncrib, and the preacher and Jed left by the light of the moon.

I stood between the barn and the corncrib. I heard Addie crying during the night, and I wanted so bad to comfort her. There was one thing that kept clamoring at my mind. *Who could do such a thing happen? And what a terrible time for them to do so.*

Chapter 17

By the time Addie came out of the crib the next morning, I had found a cast iron skillet, pitted from the heat, and cleaned it up as best I could. A part of a hog's jowl hung in the smoke house attached to the corncrib. I took my pocketknife and trimmed some meat and laid it in the skillet and set it on a bed of coals. It started to sizzle, and I slipped in the chicken house. I put my hand under a hen and pulled out two eggs and then two more from the next hen. At least there was food to eat.

All day people brought in odd pieces of furniture. Jed brought a chair. A couple of rungs were missing, and it was wobbly. But I told him I could whittle down some wood to fit it and thanked him. A family brought in a few jars of jelly and some Irish potatoes left from last year's planting. I pulled the sprouts off them and put them in the corner of the crib. Someone gave two more tickings for mattresses, and I told them I would go up to the stand of pines higher on the mountain and put in pine needles. They would do nicely.

Addie sat by the door to the crib and watched it all without speaking unless spoken too. It was too much an effort for her to make conversation with them, but everyone seemed to understand. They would pat her on the shoulder and move on. *How do you comfort someone when there are no words that can do it?*

When everyone left, I whittled on the chair rung and fixed up other pieces of cast off furniture so it would be usable. Addie stared into the clouds. She occasionally hummed a lullaby, and I knew she was thinking about Clare. Davie would throw rocks or climb a tree but did not talk to either of us. It was a day for mourning.

The ashes hid a few more pieces of usable iron cookware and a hammer with the wood handle burned away. An occasional fork, spoon, or knife was found, warped from the heat but still practical until something better could be gotten. The wind swirled ashes like dust and covered the leaves and the other buildings. A good rain would help matters a little.

I welcomed sundown. I wanted to sleep and forget for a spell.

A little past midnight, Addie took a coughing spell. I jumped the last three steps of the ladder from the loft in my haste to get to her. She was sitting by the fire on a log. She was rocking back and forth, still coughing.

"Addie, are you alright?"

"It's that smoke and ashes from today, all caught in my throat. Can't seem to get it loose."

I sat down by her on the log and, once she stopped coughing, we sat in silence.

"I dreamt about her tonight. She was in the house, and it was a-burning so high I couldn't get past the flames. I tried and tried. Woke myself up coughing from the smoke that I thought I was a-fighting. Poor Clare was just begging me to get her out of there." She choked on the words. Tears ran down her face.

I reached out and put my arm around her and pulled her head down to my lap. "I am so sorry about Clare and the fire. Both are hard to live through, and both in the same day. It weights a mind down with about more than it can bear." I patted her shoulder and finally just rubbed her arm until the snubbing and crying eased.

Addie raised her eyes to me. "Can you just stay with me tonight? Us just sit by the fire. If I sleep again, I might dream about her.

It would be fine if I could just see her a-playing or something, but see her in a fire or as a corpse. It would be more than I can bear tonight."

"Sure thing. Just rest right here." I rubbed her arm again and she fell asleep in my lap. What I really wanted to do was to take her inside the crib and lay her down to rest. Maybe even just lay down beside her so as she wouldn't feel alone. But it wasn't right. She would never care for a man that tried to take advantage. And I realized I did want her to care for me like I was beginning to care for her.

She stirred before dawn, raised up and looked me in the eyes. "You are a good man, Nathe Millsaps. They don't breed your kind of man in these parts." Her smile made my heart quiver.

"How are you feeling?"

"Stiff, but much better. The cough seems to be gone. Before I slept last night, I just told myself. 'The Lord gives, and the Lord takes away. Blessed be the name of the Lord. I will get up this morning, cook breakfast for my son and for Nathe. One foot will follow the other, and I will keep on walking.' Nothing else to do, I don't reckon."

She rose and began to gather things together for breakfast while I got the fire burning.

xxx

After breakfast, Addie and Davie went back to the corncrib. The door was open, and I could see her and Davie stretched out on the pine needle ticking. They were talking. A child-like laugh echoed out the door. It was good to hear Davie laugh. It was the first time I had heard him do that since before Clare got sick.

All day, I walked around the remains of the house, kicking ashes and pieces of planks charred from the fire. Some were splintered where they had fallen from the top of the house. Broken dishes, a thimble, a poker from the pile of rocks where the fireplace had been. A candlestick, any belongings that might still be useable. Not much was there. Objects that held memories of her husband and daughter were all gone. Possessions to make her dreams of having her own home were lost and only a pile of ashes.

A pine cone rolled under my foot, and I jumped to the side. I picked it up and could see where pine sap pitch had been dabbed in the cone. I sat down at the foot of the oak tree and looked around. Not one pine tree in sight. This was the way whoever had burnt the house had set it on fire. I looked around near the tree where I was sitting, and there was a pile of six or eight more cones, all pushed full of pine sap.

Who did it? I thought back to Amps down by the river bank cooking that fish…using pine cones to start his fire and to keep it going.

Was it him? No. He had been at the funeral while we were laying Clare in the ground. He would not have had time to get back up there by the time we saw the smoke.

Do I mention this to Addie? It was best not to do that now. It would have made no difference. Everything was lost, no matter the reason. She and Davie moved things around in the corncrib and took one of the mattress ticks and went to the pine grove and stuffed it full of needles for Davie to have his own bed.

I left the pine cones where I found them and dug through more ashes and parts of the house for anything that might still be useful.

Another day was gone, and I longed for the dark and sleep. Addie had left a pot of beans on the fire and there was fried cornbread stacked in a gourd near the fire. She and Davie were already inside with the corn crib door shut by the time I went to the barn.

I had just gotten my britches off when Addie commenced to screaming. Dreams again? I ran to the corn crib. She was trying to get the door open, and I jerked it loose. She fell on the ground, crying and pulling Davie down with her.

"Addie, there is no fire. It's just a dream." She was shaking her hands as though she was trying to get something off them and moaning. She jumped up and took Davie by the hand and drug him to the log.

"I know there ain't no fire." She screamed.

She pulled her gown up to her knees and rubbed her toes. In the light of the fire, I could see tiny bloody bites on her big toe.

"Rats, I am telling you. Dangfur rats. Eating at my feet." She screamed again and shook all over like horse trying to rid himself of his saddle.

"Rats bit you?" I ran to the oak tree and took one of the pine-tar cones and stabbed a limb into it. I held it over the coals until it flamed and made a bright light. Inside the corncrib, just at the foot of her pine needle mattress, were a few tiny grains of corn.

"They thought your toes were corn." I yelled to her.

"I don't give a rat's behind what they was a thinking." She screamed again.

I couldn't stand it any longer and began to laugh loud.

"What are you laughing about, confound you Nathe Millsaps? It ain't funny one bit." She picked up a corncob and threw it at me.

"I'm sorry, but it is funny to me."

"I hate rats. Hate 'em. Hate 'em. Hate 'em. Those little beady eyes and sharp teeth. Coming out only in the dark. Ugly creatures. Why in tarnation would God make rats?"

I didn't think she was expecting an answer.

"You and David go and sleep in my bed in the loft. I ain't seen no rats there. Not to say there ain't nairn."

"We'll do it. Probably ain't none there. Nothing would take a bite of you."

"Haaaaa. You are probably telling nothing but the truth. I will get in the crib in the morning and make sure every grain of corn is out of there. We can shake out the beds, and I will try to make up some clay and daub it in any holes so they won't be getting to you. I might even try to get a cat. Saw an old mama cat with kittens at a house up the road about six miles. I will see if they will let me have one." I didn't tell her it was at Aunt Corsie's. It would be a good excuse to see her again.

She shook again, this time like Maude after a rain shower, and took Davie to the barn with her.

xxx

The next morning I headed up to Aunt Corsie's in search of a cat. The mud daubing could wait till later in the day.

"Hello there."

"It's you again." Eliza spun around on her heel from where she was weeding the garden.

'Is your mama around?"

"She might be? I know who you are."

"My name is Nathe Millsaps. Pleased to see you again."

"You ain't Nathe Millsaps, you are Nathe Watson. My cousin.

Aunt Corsie came out of the house and spit off the porch. "Come on up here. She's too smart for her own good. But then she wouldn't be a Watson, if she wasn't so durn smart, now would she? She figured it out the time you were here before."

I sat down on the step and Aunt Corsie looked at me from head to toe. "You look like you get fed enough. Put on a little weight since you've been here, hadn't you?" She didn't wait for an answer. "Cozying right up to that widow woman I hear. Does she know who you really are yet?"

"There's no cozying being done. My real name wouldn't mean nothing to her no way. She don't know me."

"Don't be so sure, boy...There might be things you don't know about her neither."

"What you need from us? You being here could make it hard on us." Eliza yelled. She left the garden and came and stood by the steps.

"I didn't come for no reason but to ask you about that mama cat I seen running around here. Got kittens that look like they old enough to wean? I need one, if you do."

"Just an excuse. What you need with an old cat anyways?" Eliza watched me with a little less hatred than last time.

"I guess you all heard that Addie's house burnt?"

"Addie huh? Yeah heard about it. Heard that it was a set fire."

"What do you know about that?" I was careful to not be overly anxious to Aunt

Corsie, or she would close up tight like a tick on a dog and I would never get nothing from her.

"Not much really. Just said that little girl of hers had the fever and they was afraid it would spread like it did a few years ago. Killing families right hand over left. We lost five babies on this mountain five summers ago to the fever.

"Who is 'they'?"

She looked at me and narrowed her eyes. "Don't rightly know. Word of mouth, maybe. Not sure where it started."

"It ain't true you know. She did not have the fever. She had the runs, a bloody flux by the time it ended. Never could get past it. She got weaker and weaker." I folder my arms and stared at her. "Why would anyone burn the house? Didn't she have enough to worry about with a sickly child?"

"I told you why."

I looked at Eliza. "Have you been talking, girl? Did you tell them I am back? Maybe they burned it because of me. The Hoopers are trying to find me." Eliza didn't back down when I stood with my face almost against hers. She didn't say a word. I felt her fast breathing against my nose.

Aunt Corsie jerked me back around to face her. "No. It was the reason I told you. They were trying to keep us here on the mountain safe. They might have thought somebody brought in a disease. But more than likely they thought the girl had the fever. You been gone a long while, and a person with the fever could wipe out about half the people or more on this mountain if it got out amongst the people.

"That don't make no sense."

Aunt Corsie poked me in the chest. "Nothing hardly ever makes sense in these mountains. You know that. But what does make sense is to burn a house down when everything in it could cause the fever to be passed around. It would be better off burnt than us all getting it. I know that woman lost all she had. But the girl was dead. It could save the widow's life and ours if the house burnt. A few worldly belongings is worth nothing if people are dying."

"If it was catching, it would have been too late for Addie, Davie, and me. Do they want to kill us now, too? So we don't spread what they think is the fever? Why didn't they ask someone? Wouldn't it be better to find out the truth before they go destroying everything a person owns? Nobody come and asked what she died from. Not nary a person. The truth. That is what theys should have been looking for."

"You're too young and foolish to judge. You ain't never married. Ain't never had no children. I tell you we just thought that we were saving the lives of our own children."

"Well are they going to kill us too like I said? Answer me that. Cause we just might be carrying that fever right now. Brought it right here to your house to you and your daughter."

"Tell me that ain't so, Nathe. You haven't brung that fever into us have you? If so, I would have hoped that there fire had gotten you too."

"I told you there weren't no fever. She died of the trots. And she was vomiting until she just got too weak to live."

It was the look on her face that did it. And the recollection that she had said 'we were saving the lives of our children'. She was the one that had started the fire. I might not could prove it, but I believed it with everything in me.

Eliza went to the back of the house and came back with a kitten in her hand. "Take this one. It's the runt. But I know it can already catch a mouse. I seen it do it. Now a rat might be different, but it will grow some. Rats will run just because it's there, I suppose." She handed it to me. "Just take it, and get on out of here."

Aunt Corsie put her hands on her hips, "Ask that widow woman if maybe she has something she needs to tell you? Or I could just tell you."

"I don't want to hear anything you got to say. Not one word. I am taking the cat, and thank you for it. Otherwise, I will just be on my way. Glad I kept the name Milsaps. Don't think I want to be Watson anyway."

They were on the porch watching me leave, as I walked through the pine thicket out onto the road.

XXX

Addie took the cat from me and rubbed it until it purred. I threw all the pine-pitched pine combs as far as I could throw them. *My own family. How could they?* It would do no good to tell Addie who I felt had done it. It was over and done with, and it couldn't be proven anyways. I didn't want to believe it so much, that I let my mind take up the thought again that perhaps it really was a Hooper. That they might know who I was. Of course, no one had said a word, and I figured something like that would have gotten out if they thought I was a Watson. It might be time to check into what Inola had told me that day. Maybe I needed to find Levi Hooper now. My plans for revenge had been on hold long enough. The summer's harvest was almost to an end. I could take care of them and be gone by the start of winter.

Davie and I spent the rest of the day stacking the rocks of the fireplace in a pile. Hopefully we could build again, and these could be used in the new chimney.

Chapter 18

The preacher told us on the second Sunday
morning after the fire to be prepared a week
from Monday for a few families to come and
help rebuild the cabin. Any day that I wasn't
dealing with rats or helping Addie through the
day, I cut logs and snaked them in with
Maude. I made them ready for grooving and
notching to build the house. I took the last of
the money I had brought from Tennessee and
bought a load of lumber so the house would
have wood floors instead of dirt. It was a
surprise for Addie. A voice in my ear argued
that I was being foolish, and that I would need
it to leave when my revenge was done. But all
I could see was Clare and her sick in the old

drafty house. I didn't want Addie or Davie to get sick, if I could stop it.

The preacher and I spent several days hand-splitting shingles for the roof, scoring them, and placing them on end to drain, and then trimming them off. We took roosting planks from the chicken house and any scrap lumber I could find and made shutters that we would put on the windows before winter. More than likely, I would be long gone by then, but at least Addie would have a way to hold in the heat until things could be done better.

Just like the preacher said, five families came on Monday. Five men, their wives and children, and a couple of the families had two grown sons with them. The men talked with me about what was planned for the size of the house and how it was to sit.

The men and I went to the barn and pulled out the wagon loaded with planks I had hired to be planed at the lumber mill in Tuckasegee. The women folk got off their wagons and brought baskets of food to the corn crib and gave them to Addie. She wiped tears as she placed the food inside to be stored until dinner time.

We positioned stones for the foundation. Chunks of wood flew into the air from two men with axes making notches in the logs to fit them together. They were quick and direct with every swing of the axe. Two other men and me were picking up the logs and placing them. The house was taking shape in a timely manner. As soon as we completed the north and south walls, Andy began to build chimneys on each end of the house. It was determined that the house would be two rooms with an open hall between. One side would be a bedroom and sitting room on the bottom and with bedrooms half the width of the room above. The other side would be a kitchen with a loft room for a possible bedroom late, if it was needed.

Dinner was done by rotation, so the work never stopped. I piled my food onto a cracked plate that we had pulled from the ashes, stained by the heat but reasonably serviceable. I placed my plate on the back of the wagon and ate. Addie came and stood by me.

"I sent word to Papa about the fire and just got word back. He was sure sorry about my loss, Clare and the house, and was glad I had someone here to hope me. I told him I never would have made it without you. He wants to meet you when he gets back to thank you himself. They wanted to come home to be here for the rebuilding of the house but can't. Rutha lost a lot of blood and is too weak to tend to her baby.

"It will be good to meet your parents, Addie. I guess even a grown woman would want her mama at a time like this. You are about the strongest woman I ever knew."

Addie squeezed her eyes tight and bent her head. A tiny tear slid down her nose and dripped into the ashes at her feet. "I don't feel strong at all Nathe. Not atall. But I guess a soul has to just get up every day and put one foot in front of the other and go on. I just try to stay busy with the work at hand and occupy my mind. This life can be hard and demanding enough to keep us pretty much too tired to think. I just tell myself that there is nothing given to us that we are not able to bear. It's then I know I *will* find the strength to go on."

I wanted to pick her up and tell her she never had to worry about hunting strength. It was right here holding her up. I would be her strength. But like the preacher said, Addie was an upstanding woman and would not take kindly to any improper acts. It didn't keep me from wanting to do it, though.

Addie raised her eyes and looked at me. Her chest heaved and she bent forward toward me. I reached out and grabbed her arm, brushing my shoulder against her breast. I wanted to just stand there and let her lean on me. My hand reached out to touch her hair.

A man yelled from the side of the house. "Nathe. Can you hand me up some rocks for the chimney?"

I had forgotten the others were anywhere around. It had been just me and Addie in my mind. She raised her head from my shoulder. I dropped my hands but looked into her eyes. "Sure enough. I will be right there."

Addie turned and looked toward the house that was near to being built.

"'I'll be here, Addie. If there is anything you need, I want to take care of it. You've been through a lot in your life. Lost a husband, a baby girl, a home. It ain't right for a woman like you to have to endure this much. I...."

"Go and help with the house, Nathe. We will talk later."

When the walls were head high, the women and children took chunks of the wood left from notching and stuffed them into the cracks between the logs. Just after dinner, the preacher came with a load of clay to which we added water until it was sticky. Women and children shoved it into the cracks until the air holes within their reach were chinked.

I watched the people working around me. We all had the same portion in life, endured the same hardships. We shared the same sicknesses and fears. No one's clothes were fancier than their neighbors. People just trying to get by. If we kindled a fire, anyone was welcome to sit by it. Like Amps had welcomed me that first night here. Addie had said those very words. It made life make sense. Speaking of Amps, where had he been during the building of the room? I asked a few people and no one seemed to recall anyone by that name. It was hard to figure a way to say where he lived without calling it the Watson place and them wondering how I knew that. They might figure it was common knowledge, but what if they didn't... I held back my questions.

The next day they all came back, along with two more families. It would take several more men to get the logs above the height of the day before and to put on the rafters and roof.

The men started the roof and were finished before dark. They quickly packed up their axes and tools and hurried home before the sun set.

xxx

Addie was disappointed that I decided not to go to church on Sunday. "After all they have done for me and for you. They are good people. I don't understand why you won't go today."

"I am not feeling well."

She looked in my eyes. "Do you have a fever? Anything else ailing you? I don't want you getting sick on me."

It was a lie. It didn't feel good lying to her, but I sure couldn't tell her what I had planned. "I think if I just lay down. I will feel better by tomorrow. Can you and Davie drive the wagon?"

"Of course. We did it before you came. I hope you feel better." She appeared to have accepted my excuse.

The week before, I had sold three bushel of corn to the preacher to feed to his horse. I took the money down to the store in East Laporte and asked if they knew of somebody that might have a cow that I could buy. If only I could have gotten the cow earlier, then maybe Clare would have been healthier and could have fought off the sickness. I felt guilty. There was money in my bag that I could have used but saved it for myself and waited until Addie might get the money. It was easy to talk to myself about how I needed to be careful with what money I had so that I could get away when the time came. But to keep something from a little girl that could have made her healthier, and then she up and died…

All the years of planning and finding ways to soothe my conscience with the thought of the justice that I would provide made it easier than it should have been to carry out today's act. I did plan to buy a cow, but the real reason was to pretend that someone told me to go to Levi Hooper's house to ask him. I needed to look in his face.

The store was closed on the Sabbath, but Forks of the River Baptist Church was right nearby. I was there when they got out of service and planned to ask about a cow to buy. I stood by the tree in the graveyard east of the church. The door opened and children slid between their parents and into the yard to run and play before time to go home. Instead of climbing into their wagons, women carried baskets filled with food from their wagons. They spread out tablecloths into a long line and laid out food. It was a dinner on the ground.

The storekeeper from the East Laporte store attended the church and saw me standing by the tree. "Come on down, young man, and join us. There is always plenty of food."

"I don't want to be an extra mouth to feed. The only reason I am here is to see if you know anyone wanting to sell a cow. I am in the market for one."

"Son, we don't do business on the Sabbath. Why don't you come and eat and get to know some of the people, and it might be that someone can tell you a place you can find a cow to buy on Monday."

There was nothing left to do but to eat with them. What would I do if one of them was Levi Hooper? "

The food was really good. It made me realize how skimpy Addie's food supply really was. I felt guilty eating from this kind of spread with chicken and dumplings and beef and pork, and Addie and Davie at home with only vegetables and some dried jerky and maybe squirrel or rabbit on occasion.

The storekeeper's family let me sit with them on the quilt they had laid on the ground. People came by and introduced themselves. No one had the name of Hooper and I ventured a question. "I hear tell that a Levi Hooper might have a cow to sell. Do you know where he lives?"

"Well, for one thing, I never would have thought that Levi had much of anything to sell, but he lives halfway up Wayhutta mountain."

"What do you mean you don't think he would have anything to sell?"

"Well I'm not judging, but him and his family have a hard way to go and have for a number of years. Most of this is hearsay, as they haven't come to church here since...well in quite a few years. It might be unkind of me, but I think sometimes we reap what we sow.

"But don't pay me no mind. He could have several cows from what I know. You could ask Grayson Mills. He might know."

I shook my head while he was still saying the words. "No. That won't be necessary. If you can, just tell me where he lives, I'll go and ask. Getting the words from the horse's mouth is usually better. I will do it on Monday." Lies had become easy to tell. It didn't feel good in my conscience either.

"It's that lower mountain you see in the northeast. Follow Wayhutta creek to the falls and then turn directly east. He picked up his plate and went to the cakes and pies.

I felt the shopkeeper's wife eying me. "If you talk to them, will you tell Levi's wife, Polly, that I would love to see her again."

"Sure enough, ma'am."

"She's had a hard life, what with Levi being bedridden. She does pretty much all the work around that place."

"Bedridden? What brought that on?"

"It was a logging accident near Sylva. He was in a passel of people clearing for the railroad that was coming out of Asheville to

Sylva. A tree fell on him and must have
broken his back. He don't have paralysis but
not much use for his legs. They say he crawls
out on the porch and back to the bed. That's
bout the extent of his gettin' around." She
went to the food and came back with a whole
rhubarb pie and two chicken legs and two
thighs wrapped in a cloth. "We have plenty
food and as you are a single man, I want to
send some with you for later. My name is
Tincey. My son got killed in the war, and he
would have been only a few years older than
you. I would hope that someone did the same
for him when he was in some strange
country."

"Thank you ma'am." I had heard enough
about Levi, and I was excited to get alone and
make some plans.

Her husband came back with a buttermilk
pie. "Take this to the family where you are
staying. We have more than enough to share."

I nodded, but moved away quickly. Levi
could be an easy target when I decided to
make my move. But first I wanted to see him
for myself. The only bother was that Tincey
and some others knew I had been asking about
him. But it was not likely they would ever see
me again after I killed him. I would be gone
from these mountains in two shakes of a
lamb's tail.

xxx

The directions took me right to the place. Just like Tincey said, Levi was sitting on the porch in the floor with his legs dangling off the edge.

I thought that Addie had it hard, but this place made hers look like a king's palace. The house was near about falling down. There was no animal in or around the barn that I could tell. Not even a horse. Don't guess he had no use for one as he couldn't ride. *Wonder how they're getting food?*

The shots scattered the dust near my feet, and I screamed and jumped like I was dancing. "I'm not here to do harm. Not going to steal from you either."

"Not much you could steal I don't think." Mrs. Hooper spit off the end of the porch. She reached in her mouth with her forefinger and thumb and pulled out a wad of tobacco and laid it on the window sill. "But you've no business around here or on our land. Who are you anyways?"

"My name is Nathe Millsaps. I was down at the Baptist Church at the Forks of the River and someone by the name of Tincey asked if I would bring this to you." The lies tasted bitter in my mouth…the food and the promise to do no harm. I reasoned that Tincey liked Mrs. Hooper as she has spoken kindly when she talked about her. If she had known I was coming, she would have surely sent it to them.

It didn't sound any truer in my mind as I tried to make the lie more tasty.

"Tincey, eh. That was real Christian of her."

Levi did not speak. He had not looked our way until I mentioned the food. I eased my way to the porch and handed her the food. She grabbed it at the same time as Levi, and the pieces of chicken fell on the porch. One grabbed a leg and the other a thigh and tore at the meat. Both of their teeth were broken or completely missing in the front. Levi took his tongue and reached as far as he could to wipe every drop of grease from around his mouth.

Mrs. Hooper grabbed the pie and stepped away from the edge of the porch.

"Give me that pie." Levi leaned backward and took a hold of his wife's ankle.

"You'll get your share. Just give me a minute." She grabbed the crust in two hands and broke it in half. She handed him his share.

It was something about their desperate fight over the food that did it. Killing him would not satisfy my need for revenge. This would be too easy. It needed to be a full-bodied man so that the death would be felt and mourned deeply. These were a forgotten people. Starvation would get them in no time. *Ain't there no family left to care enough to make sure they have food?* He couldn't be more than forty-eight years old but he looked seventy, if he looked a day.

My feelings of sympathy angered me. I didn't have any concern for a Hooper. Let them starve. But I had to find someone to kill

that would make a bigger blow on the Hoopers
than a worn-out old man.

"I best be on my way. Have a good day.'

Mrs. Hooper laughed without any sound
of happiness. "Did you hear that Levi? He told
us to have a good day. When was the last time
we had a good day, do you think? I can't
remember the last time anyone said for us to
have one either."

I looked at her. *What else do I say?*
Should I tell her, 'it may be the best day of your
life', as I have decided not to kill you'. But I
was not sure that might not be the kindest
thing to do…to kill them and get them out of
their misery.

"I thank ye fer the food, man."

It was strange to hear him speak. His
voice was coarse and forced out from deep in
his throat. The effort made him have a
coughing spell. His wife began to beat him on
the back as he gasped for air. I walked to the
road and stood behind a tree until his coughing
stopped. One last look, and I saw him pull his
limp body with his arms and hands toward the
door of the house.

Running robbed me of my air, but I did
not stop until I was a mile from the house. I
slid my back down a tree and put my head
between my knees. Was Addie that close to
starving when the church brought her food
right before I came? If they had been two
weeks later would I have found her and the
kids dead? Her family had not checked on her

since I had been around, although I did know she got letters they sent from someone down at the church. But she was the kind that would never tell anyone her needs unless it was her family. It made me sick to my stomach when I pictured Addie and the children fighting over a few morsels of food.

It was harder than I had expected. I thought I could find a Hooper, shoot him, and be on my way. Why did it have to be like this? A deathly sick man, some stranger that acted like he knew all about me and trying to get me to change my way of thinking, a woman and two kids that I felt responsible for. It was too hard. Why did I come back? I would to God that I had stayed in Tennessee.

Chapter 19

I awoke to Davie and Addie talking outside the corncrib. I peeked out through a crack and could see them pulling out the furniture that had been given to her when she moved into the makeshift home. She was excited to get into her new house.

The men from the church had left me to put down the lumber for the floors, and it was now done.

"Davie, get that fire going, and heat water to wash the furniture down. Where did I put that lye soap the preacher brought to us? I don't want to put dirty furniture into that clean, new house." She was smiling from ear to ear.

I left the barn still buttoning my shirt. "You sure are getting an early start."

"Well the daylight is a wasting. We have lots to do to get into the house."

"You are going to be needing more furniture."

"Papa and Mama are coming today. They're bringing some furniture too. I got a letter from them yesterday at church.

It was clear she was excited about seeing her family. "That will be a fine treat for you Addie. I am a-glad they're coming. What furniture you don't have here and what they don't bring, I will see about me making it for you, if I can."

Addie's face turned red. Her head was slightly bent, and she looked up through her eyelashes at me. "You really are a mighty fine man. You couldn't be better to me if'n you were my husband. I don't know what we would have done without you. I hate it that you're sleeping in that old barn. You deserve a bed and a nice nightstand with a lamp on it."

"I'm fine for the time being. There will come a day for that, I'm a-hopin'."

Addie looked back toward the house. "This is kind of strange. It feels like we are a newlywed couple and setting up housekeeping. It feels like it did that day that Ashe and I came up here with his papa in a wagon with what furniture Mama and Papa had given me.

They showed me the house and what they had given Ashe to set up housekeeping with. Now I feel like I am a young bride with everything new and fresh. My life just beginning."

"Well, you are getting to start again in a new house. I am sorry you lost all those memories with Ashe, though. It can't be easy."

"Mama, if'n I wash this here table anymore it will be water-logged. Can I stop now?"

We both laughed, and I reached out and tousled Davie's hair. "I don't think it's near being water-logged, boy. Scrub her down good for yore ma. She has to have the house nice for when you grandpa and grandma get here."

It just didn't seem right to start back the conversation we were having at that moment, so I went to the corncrib to get the rest of their things to move to the house.

xxx

It was about sundown when I watched Addie jump from the top step of the porch and run toward the dust that was swirling into the air about an eighth mile down the road.

"It's Papa and Mama. I know it has to be."

"They won't be getting here any faster with you running to the road." I yelled at her girlish form as she rushed toward them.

"No, but I will see them sooner." She stopped and looked back at me. "I haven't seen Papa nor Mama in over six months. Papa was ill and didn't want the children to be near him in case they caught the sickness. Then Sister got pregnant. She always was sickly, and they have traveled to Asheville two times to be with her. I miss them terribly."

My heart lurched inside of me at the sad look on her face. "Well run on and see them, girl."

She smiled real big, then jerked up her dress tail in her hands and run.

Davie was sitting in the swing. "Are you not running too?"

"Naw. They'll be here when they get here, I reckon. I'll just sit here on the porch."

"Well scoot over, and I will wait with you.

"What's your Grandpa like?"

Davie grinned. "He's a lot like you. Quiet most of the time, but when he does speak, it seems to always help a person."

I never knew he felt like that about me. "Well he must be a fine man to have a daughter like Addie and a grandson like you."

"And a granddaughter like Clare. He loved Clare. I bet it was hard on him not to be here for her burying. She was the apple of his eye. He took it hard when we moved back here to this house. She was his favorite."

"I am sure he loved you all. You was probably a lot of help to him when you lived there."

"Some. But Uncle Pierce did most of the farming and helping Grandpa and Grandma."

Pierce! That was a common enough name in the mountains. Sure there was Pierce Hooper but when I left I also knew a Pierce Mills and a Pierce Johnson. My heart slowed down at bit at my own reasoning.

Davie couldn't contain himself any longer. He jumped up and ran toward the wagon. "Grandpa. It's about time you come home."

Addie was sitting between her Mama and Papa. She held her Mama's hand, and her head was on her papa's shoulder. I hadn't seen her that happy since Clare was gone. In fact, I don't think I ever saw her as happy.

"Nathe, come and meet my folks. Papa and Mama, this here is Nathe Millsaps. He came over from Tennessee. He has been living in the barn. I don't think we could have made it without him these past few months.

I blushed with pleasure. "This here is my Papa, Nathe. Clay Hooper."

I stepped backward like someone had hit me with a shovel. My ears roared like the sound of locusts on a hot summer night. I stumbled toward the outstretched hand reaching off the wagon and took it. It was not easy, but I looked him straight in the eye. His hands were smooth, like he had not done any hard work in many a year. I remembered how his hands looked on the gun he had aimed at Uncle Monroe's temple. Rough and gnarled

from hard work. Now he looked old and weak.
Nothing like the last time I had seen him. He
had deep furrows at the corner of his eyes. I
always thought these lines came from a person
that laughed a lot, but his came from
narrowing his eyes like he was doing now.
"You look pale. Are you feeling poorly?" His
voice was the same as when he yelled for Levi
to grab me.

"I…No. Go on in the house. I will unhitch
your horse and feed him." I ran to the horse's
head and held the harness as they climbed
down.

"Not before we unload. If I know my
daughter, she's anxious to see what we
brought. Say you're from Tennessee? What
brings you to these mountains?"

I swallowed at the lump stuck in my
throat. It was a little easier to talk with the
space between us from the horse's head and
where he was unloading the back of the
wagon, pulling out an iron skillet and iron
dutch oven. A white oak basket had odds and
ends of dishes.

"I just needed a change of scenery. I like
the mountains."

"Well you won't find a fuss with me. I
wouldn't live any place else. Can you come
and help me unload this rocker and bedstead?"
He pulled it to the edge of the wagon bed.

It would have been strange to refuse. We
unloaded the heavy things. Then I jumped into
the wagon and handed down bed slats and rails

for two beds and various other household items.

Addie acted like nothing was amiss and continued to talk to her mother. "How is Rutha, Mama?"

"Ah honey she is just doing poorly, but we left her a little better than we found her. She should have never had a baby. She's too peaked to require her body have to support her and a baby at the same time. But what can a woman do? That's what we are put on this earth for...to bear children."

The women folk picked up the basket of dishes and skillets and went into the house. Davie took his grandpa by the hand and pulled him toward the tree house. He and I had built it last spring. We had used saplings cut from the field on the back side of Addie's land. I was getting it ready for another cornfield for next year. Then she would have enough to support not just a horse or a cow but maybe a hog or two. *What could I have been planning in the backside of my mind?* It was like I was planning on staying around and make this home. But today shook up any plans of making a family with Addie and Davie. My plans for revenge came pouring down on me like a waterfall. *Papa, I haven't forgotten, and I will not let a thing stop me from doing what a Watson man has to do.*

What I really wanted to do right now was to put as much distance between me and Addie as possible. She was a Hooper. She was my enemy. Oh, I knew that no women folk had been in on the murders but still… There could never be anything between us. Nothing could keep me from doing what I had to do. It was the reason I came back. My entire life had been lived for this time. This act of revenge. To do otherwise was to turn my back on my family. I couldn't do that.

Could I really go in that house and pretend nothing was wrong? That I was just Nathe Millsaps, a man from Tennessee. A good man that was helping Addie. Nothing more. I had to. At least for a short time.

I stuck my head inside the door of the kitchen where Mrs. Hooper was putting up dishes. "Ma'am, your wagon is unloaded, and the horse is in the stable. I gave him some corn and hay."

"Well, thank ye, Nathe. You sure did a good job on the new cabin. It's so big and roomy. It will make a nice home for my daughter and Davie. Maybe even a bigger family." She looked at Addie and grinned. Addie flushed bright red and looked at me and smiled a timid smile. Her mother laughed out loud.

I turned my head and refused to look at Addie any more.

"We are going to fix supper, and you will come in here and eat with us. I sent Clay out to kill that chicken I brought in the coop. Nice fresh fried chicken and mashed taters will make a hearty meal."

"And blackberry cobbler too, right Grandma?"

She rubbed his hair. "You can count on it, David Thomas. Just for you."

"I'll go outside and get the taters from the cellar." I saw Addie's face as I turned. She looked hurt. It couldn't be helped. It was best to not let her think there could ever be anything between us. Up until now, it had been in the back of her mind just like it had mine.

I made it through supper as I listened to the loving conversations between their family, but left as soon as I could.

I went to the barn and grabbed my pack.

Out of the darkness I heard, "Nathe."

I pushed the pack into a corner. "Yeah."

Addie climbed the ladder and stuck her head through the hole in the floor. "I don't understand. What is wrong? Did I do something? Did Papa or Mama do something?"

"There is nothing wrong. You all are family. I'm an outsider."

"No, Nathe, you're not an outsider. You are a part of the family. You were here and took care of me when Clare died. Without you, I wouldn't have food in the cellar or corn in the crib or hay in the barn from the spring cutting. My house would be gone and I'd have no wheres to live. You worked hard for all this."

I could see her outline. She was so pretty in the moonlight that came through the open shutters on the end of the barn.

"I think of you as family. Don't you feel it?" She motioned for me to come nearer.

"Go inside Addie. We will talk later."

"Wait."

"I have something I have to do. Go back inside."

She stepped off the ladder. I hurried down and ran past her into the darkness.

xxx

I poked at the fire with the stick that Amps often used. He was not there but the fire burned brightly as it had every time I had been here at night. Spring, summer, and now fall.

My feet were sore and my breath was short. I had run almost every step since I left the house. The need to get away from there put fire in my feet.

There was something about this place that called to me to think through my problems and hoped me make decisions. Maybe it was the flames or the seclusion. It could be Amps. He seemed to know my thoughts and asked me to think differently. I didn't want to think differently tonight of all times. Ten years of dwelling on the terrible murders by the Hoopers demanded of me to put Addie and this life to the side and take care of family matters. The time it took to run from her house to here gave me time to think about what this would do to me and Addie. I knew I loved her, but it changed everything. The duty taught to me about blood kin by my family was loud in my ears, begging me for revenge. It was my responsibility.

"Looks like the devil hisself has been on your coattail, Nat." Only Mama had called me Nat. "You look all red-faced and panting for breath. What are you doing out at night? You are usually up there with that little family you have adopted. Maybe sparking a little with the widder woman…" Amps walked to the fire and poured a cup of coffee in a tin cup and handed it to me. His bony frame stood over me.

"Stop it, Amps. You don't know nothing about me or what I do up at Addie's. You sit down here around your campfire and think you know everything there is to know. Only time you are anywhere else that I ever seen is when you show up following me somewhere that I don't want you with me. Like hunting…but without a gun. Or fishing…with no pole in your hand. You think you know about me. But you don't. Do you hear? I am not what anybody thinks I am."

"How do you know what I think you are? You may be secretive but you show yourself in things you say and places you go."

"How do you know where I go?"

"I know when you first came here, you headed straight up to a cabin that the Watsons lived in when some blood massacre took a bunch of them out of the world. Why would you want to do that?"

I jumped up and faced him. "How do you know I did that?"

"I have my ways of knowing. You sure are quare…never wanting anybody to know a thing about you. If you want to be that secretive, why did you go and get involved with a local widder woman? Have you told her why you are here?"

"There's no reason to tell her anything. I just work for her."

"Oh I see. You just work for her. All that time you spent looking in on her and the children, back when Clare was alive, and even now with Davie…all those times, you weren't falling in love with her? I don't believe you."

I turned my back to him and walked around the fire to the other side. "How do you know these things? Do you go a-peaking at me wherever I am? You spook me. Do you know that? You are like some kind of fool ghost."

"The point is you need to figure out exactly what you want. I think you are at some kind of crossroads, and you need to make a decision. You can't do what you may be a-feeling and still have a life with Addie."

Amps sat down on the log. I turned my back to the fire and watched his face with the flames shooting light across his aged skin, all cooked with summer heat and red from the heat of the fire. His beard had what looked like a three day growth, but it had been that length all spring and summer.

"What makes you think I am a-needing to make a decision?"

Amps didn't answer but continued to stare deep into my eyes and reach down into my thoughts. "Well, ain't ye?"

I threw the rest of the coffee in the fire and threw the cup at his feet and left.

xxx

Rain started as a slow drip but picked up as I walked back up the road. There was no wheres to go but back to the barn. It was dry and warm. It was childish to run off without any plans. Clay didn't know who I was, and I could rest in peace. They were going to stay a few days and try to help Addie set up house. There were plenty of things to keep me busy in the fields so as to not have to see them. I knew now that my time was short. Either I killed them and ran, or else I would be killed before this thing was done. At any rate, I wanted to leave Addie better off as far as food and a place to live for having known me. She would have this year's crops harvested, wood for the winter, and all the fields but one turned so as to make it easier for her and Davie in the spring.

Sleep didn't come easy. My mind was busy with too many things. When I did sleep, I dreamed. My mother was with me. I was the

age I am now, not a little boy like I would
have thought I would be in such a dream. But
she looked exactly like she did the last time I
saw her. She even had a rag tied around her
head and covering her eye. She sat and looked
at me but did not speak for the longest. Just
before I woke, she said "Nat, why do you
think I sent you away?" I told her it was to
keep me safe. She said. "That too." I wanted
to go back to sleep and see what other reason
she had sent me away other than safety. Could
there have been another reason?

xxx

The last patch of the planting ground for next
spring had been turned up by the end of the
day, mid week. The more I thought about what
I had to do, the faster I pushed Maude to go. I
had to find out who was still alive and who
was already passed on. I could kill the son of
one of the others that had passed, but it would
not bring the heartache as some Hooper that
still had plenty of living relatives to grieve. It
was dangerous to do it that way, but more
satisfying. The thought passed through my
mind of killing ever living Hooper I could
find, but that did not suit my need for their
family to mourn. But a multiple funeral like
ours could make me feel justice had been
performed.

Now all I had to do was to get them talking about their family and who was alive and who was dead.

Chapter 20

I worked in the fields all day and stayed clear of the family reunion inside the house.

I took supper that night with Addie and her family, so as to not raise any suspicions. I kept quiet and listened. They talked about how Clay's son, Pierce, had died in the war and had never married. It hadn't entered my mind to go down to the Hooper Cemetery to see if there were any graves marked with the ones that did the killing. I found, that by keeping quiet, I learned pretty much everything I wanted to know.

Their cousin, Silas Beck, was a possibility until Davie asked his grandfather a question.

"Grandpa, tell me again what happened to Silas."

Addie waved at her Papa to stop. "Davie, I don't like you hearing these stories. I just hate it…hate it all. The killing, the feuding, and the drinking. I want all these happening to never be spoken of again."

Clay snapped back at his daughter, "I know you don't like it, and I guess I understand why, now that I am old. But the boy has a right to know about his family, and how they died. The only way a person lives awhile after his death is for someone to speak his name from time to time. Once no one remembers, and the rocks in the cemetery crumble, they are truly gone. Gone forever."

Clay's eyes had tears in them. "Someday soon, I'll be gone. You know me and will talk about me. Davie will remember me I think and call my name with some memory. But after that, Clay Hooper, will not be referred to, as me, ever again. It's just sad to think about."

"Papa, you still have lots of time…"

"It's not true, Addie girl. You have to think about that. You really need a good man to take care of you and give you more children. I want to live to see that happen. I really do. Then I can rest in peace I think."

Clay looked me square in the eye. I looked away. "A papa needs to know his daughters are taken care of."

He wouldn't want me to be that man if he knew who I really was. There was no doubt about that. But by the time he found out, I would be long gone or dead...whichever luck would have it.

"Grandpa, tell me about Silas. Please."

"Silas learned doctoring during the war. When he came back, he took his family and moved across the mountains to Tennessee. He said he saw things a lot clearer while he was in the War. I heard that a whole town was almost wiped out by cholera, and he worked till he died moving from one house to the next to treat the patients. I went to the funeral. He had some children over there, but I ain't heard anything from them since Silas died."

Clay was in front of me. Pierce died in the war without issue. Silas died in Tennessee with Cholera. There were still Levi's sons perhaps, if he had any. *How am I going to find that out?*

I thought from one family to the next. "You have had quite a large size family, sounds like. Are there others that live around here?"

Addie, glad that I was finally taking part in the family talks, spoke up. "Papa has a younger brother by the name of Levi. He's a cripple, both in body and mind."

"But surely some of these left children...cousins? I thought family kept close ties in these mountains. Ain't it true?"

Addie hesitated. "Levi has two sons. They are both in prison somewhere in Virginia."

Mrs. Hooper patted Addie's hand. "Honey child, I really dread leaving here tomorrow and going home. All you have gone through. My, my, my. Our family is cursed with tragedy it seems. That sweet baby Clare."

Addie started to cry.

"Oh child, I didn't say it to make you cry. I just needed to say her name. I am so glad you have Nathe here with you. I truly am." She looked at me. "Son, you are crying too. You must have loved that little girl. But then everybody did. From the day she was born, she was special. Should have known she was not long on the earth. She was just an angel.

"Addie, you dry those eyes. She is up there with her Papa, and he has to be rocking her and telling her all about how much he loves you. Then my Papa and Mama are there, too. They will take good care of her till we all meet again. Your Papa and me listened to the best sermon at our church about how our loved ones are just awaiting for us up there. It makes you plum homesick."

Clay stood up and came to his wife's side. "That's enough weeping. We need to think about packing our stuff up so as we can leave at daybreak. We haven't seen Marshall since we came back from Rutha's. He turns twenty-six in four days, and I want to be there on his birthday. Want to see little Glee." Clay looked at me. "If he didn't go and name him after me. Glee Clay Hooper.

"They will be home tomorrow, Marshall said, but on his birthday he has to take his wheat to the mill."

It was then that I knew that Marshall was the one to die. Maybe even Glee. Well, no…Maybe let Glee live but with the same memory as me…living with no Papa. Knowing that Marshall was killed because his grandpa Clay Hooper was a murderer. That would make things right for the Watsons.

xxx

The barn didn't seem inviting to me. I had too much on my mind. Inside, they were making pallets and bedding down. Clay and Mrs. Hooper were to have Addie's bed, and she had made herself a pallet between the table and the door.

Outside, I stood with my back against the post on the porch and watched them. Davie was talking to his Grandma.

"Grandma, if some woman wanted a man, what are some of the things she could do to get one?

"Why are you wanting to know about a woman getting a man? Shouldn't you be wondering how to get a girl for yourself?"

"Lord have mercy, I don't want no girl. I was thinking about Mama."

"So you think yore mama needs a man?"

"Well, she does need one. She just don't know it. We need to be a family. Even

Grandpa says she needs someone to take care of her. Someday I will be grown and won't be here."

Mrs. Hooper looked at Addie who smiled and shook her head in amazement. "So you want me to tell you some of my sure-fire ways for husband hunting? I can do that. Now you realize yore Mama might not use them, right? But anyway I will tell you, just in case."

"Thank you Grandma. I told Clare one time that I would ask you, and you would tell us."

Grandma grabbed Davie and hugged him. Addie was dabbing tears from the corners of her eyes. "You really were a Friday's child, Davie. I was right here when you were born."

"What's a Friday's child?"

Grandma recited the saying. "Monday's child is fair of face; Tuesday's child is full of grace; Wednesday's child is full of woe; Thursday's child has far to go; Friday's child is loving and giving; Saturday's child works hard for a living. But the child that is born on the Sabbath day is fair and wise, good, and gay."

Addie reached over her mother's shoulder and took her hand. "Clare was a Tuesday's child. So graceful. So lovely. So sweet."

Grandma nodded and wiped tears too.

"What about those potions or ways to get a man?" Davie piped in. "Grandpa, make them tell me."

The women laughed. Clay was already snoring in Addie's bed.

"Very well. Let me think a minute. Now, Davie, you ain't swept under yore mama's feet have you?"

He shook his head hard. "I don't sweep."

"Alright then, we got that taken care of. If someone sweeps under your feet, you'll never marry. Then hang a pulley bone over the front door, and the first man who passes under it is the man your mama will marry."

I could see Davie thinking deep on this one. He knew I was the only unmarried man that would come in that door. The only one that had, since I had been here.

Davie jumped in excitement. "I had the pulley bone for supper. I will hang it."

What about this one, son? If a kettle of hot water is poured over the doorstep and a woman walks through it, there will be wedding in that house within the year."

Davie yawned. "Can we do that first thing tomorrow?"

"We surely can, son. Now let's all go to bed."

I sat down under the window underneath where Addie lay on a quilt in the floor. I couldn't see her, but she was talking softly. *"This Friday night while going to bed, I put my petticoat under my head, To dream of the living and not of the dead, To dream of the man I am to wed. The color of his eyes, the color of his hair, The color of the clothes he is to wear."*

It all made me very sad. All this wanting things from life that would never happen.

I went to the barn. Addie's brother was the only living person other than Clay that I could use to carry out my plan. It would be hard on Addie, but it would have to be that way. If only I had never stayed here in the barn and gotten to know her. She was nothing like what I thought a Hooper would be.

"Nathe." Addie stuck her head up through the hole in the barn loft. "Can I come up for a little while?"

Why couldn't I say no to her? I needed to make my feelings for her die. She would hate me when it was over and done. She wouldn't be able to understand why I had to do it.

Addie crawled off the ladder and came and sat on the hay beside my bed. I wouldn't look at her but could feel her staring at me.

"What's it like out there, Nathe?"

"Out where?"

"Out there beyond these mountains. I never lived anywhere but right here in Jackson County. It never made any sense to me that there were other places to live. Mama and Papa live here, and everyone that I love does too. So what is it like? You've lived out there. A long ways away. In Tennessee."

"Tennessee is really not that far away."

"To me it is. It's beyond the mountains. Another world. Ashe wrote me letters and

described places. He wrote me from
Cumberland Gap. Right there where
Tennessee, Kentucky, and Virginia meet. That
was the last letter I got before he was killed.
He told me about how it was this huge flat
land you could see from the top of the Gap on
this high, high mountain. It stretched for miles
and miles. I would close my eyes and try to
imagine it. I could see it like it is raining. The
land was so flat that the water just soaked right
in and didn't make gulleys because it lay on a
sidling place. You could go to church and not
have to think about climbing up the mountain
when you came back. You probably wouldn't
even have to stop and let your horse rest like
you do here. Flat land would be nice for
planting crops I guess, but I just love finding a
place to look over the valley from up here and
see smoke blowing up from cabins and know
my family and a friends are down there
somewhere. All those mountains just a-laying
in layers all the way west into Tennessee and
all the way east to Asheville. I never been to
Asheville, but Mama and Papa have and
Rutha. They tell me about it.

"Ashe told me acres and acres of land
were cleared. In places there were hardly any
trees at all. I didn't even want to think about
that. I like the shade. There wouldn't be any
trees blowing in the wind like I love or seeing
fog roll and swirl around in the wind through
the boughs of the trees."

Her eyes were focused out the open end of the barn.

"Do the peoples talk different out there? Can you understand them real good? I know I understand you, but I figured you were probably different. Rutha wrote me and said some people there talk funny when they move into Asheville, especially if they come from up north."

I lay on my back and stared into the rafters. "People do make fun of mountain people's talk some I reckon."

"Rutha says they do. What makes one person's talk right and another one wrong? It's jest the way we say things, and their way is theirs. I can't understand them sometimes any more than they understand me, but what makes ours so wrong that they laugh? Do you think I talk funny? You sound like me. But do other people over in Tennessee, do they talk strange?"

I turned on my right side and faced her. "They talk just fine. Some say words a little different, but most of the time you can still understand them."

"Do they live like we do? What kind of houses do they live in? Are they log or cut planks with fancy things hanging on the walls? I bet they have lace curtains, and the women folks just sit and sew fancy dresses. Maybe they have so much money that they order clothes from another country through a catalog."

I rolled over on my back and put both arms behind my head and stared into the rafters. "Addie, they are just like you. Some have fancier houses, and some have houses not even as nice as yours. There are people better off than others, just like there are here."

She was not satisfied. "The only people I see much is at church, and I only know about the people whose houses I pass on the way there and back. But theirs is just like mine. We pretty much all live alike. What is different out there? What makes a person want to leave these mountains and go somewhere else?"

"Why have you becomes so interested in the world beyond here?"

"Maybe because you seem to be interested. All of a sudden, you don't seem happy here. So there must be something you're missing from over there in Tennessee. Is there another woman?"

"I have never loved another woman."

"Another? Does that mean, maybe, you love me?"

She didn't linger over the question when I didn't answer. "I know men don't use the word love like women do. We tell our children we love them, and it comes natural. Some women tell their husbands that, and I guess some men do tell their women folk, but it ain't as common. But I just wanted you to know that, if it was just Tennessee and not another woman that is making you feel like moving on, I'd be willing to leave here and go with you if you wanted. Oh, I would miss Mama and Papa, but having you would be worth it."

"Oh Addie." I could not face her.

She lay down beside me on the bed with her back to me. "I just want to stay a minute with you, if that is ok."

"It's fine."

Neither of us spoke, and, after about ten minutes, she got up and went back to the house.

Chapter 21

Addie came to the barn and yelled up into the loft for me to come to breakfast.

There was a puddle of water at the back steps with small footprints where Addie had walked. After I sat down, I looked above the door. Sure enough, there was Davie's pulley bone. Davie sat in his chair and exchanged little smiles with his Grandma.

Addie's parents left after breakfast. I brought their wagon around, said goodbye, and then made myself useful in the barn.

When they were out of sight, I came to where Addie sat on the porch.

"Your parents finally left I see."

"Yes. I sure hated to see them go. Davie rode with them down to the forks of the road, and then he will walk back."

"So they are going to your brother Marshall's house? Where exactly does Marshall live?"

"Up on Horney Head Mountain above East Laporte."

"Does he have a good house?"

"It's tolerable. Not as good as the one you built for me." She wrinkled her nose in pleasure as she looked at me. "It is two rooms but no run between them like this one. It was our Grandpa's. He has built a bigger barn. There are enough acres for him to have his own wheat and corn. He builds wagons too. Papa said he's just like our Grandpa Amos. The home place is not hard to find. It is right at the top of Horney Head Mountain at Hornbeck Gap."

"They said Marshall had to go to the mill the day of his birthday. What mill does he use?"

"East Laporte."

"I had better get back to the barn. Got some more work to do."

"I will have your dinner about noon, Nathe. When Davie gets back, make him help you work."

xxx

The rain had started coming more often, and it made the nights cool. I stood outside the barn at the end of the day after her Papa left. I watched Addie send Davie to bed and waited for her to blow out her lamp. I thought about what had been our last conversation. It was about Marshall. That would always be in her mind when she thought of me. I was not happy about that.

My backpack had it all inside. Mama's letter. A change of clothes. I had left my coat outside the pack, as I might need it in the morning when I left. For certain I needed the gun.

"Nathe."

I jumped. "Addie what are you doing out here? I thought you were in bed."

She looked at the pack in one hand and my coat and gun in the other. "What are you doing, Nathe? Are you leaving?"

I dropped my head.

"Have I done something wrong? Am I too old? Is that why you don't want to marry me?"

"You aren't too old. You're a wonderful woman. Any man would be glad to have you as a wife."

"Not you, it seems. I would like to be your wife. All I got is this rocky farmland that you have made profitable by the sweat of your brow and the blisters on your hands." She took my hands, held them in hers, and looked at them. Her lips trembled. She timidly looked up. "But the farm is yours too, if you will stay

and marry me. Nathe, will you marry me? I
ain't against asking. You have been a real
gentleman. Maybe even more than I wanted at
times. You loved my children like they were
yore own. You built my house, tended to my
fields, and laid up in store for the winter. You
already are a husband in just about every way
there is."

She turned red and I laughed softly.

"I'll be as good a wife to you as I know
how to be. Oh, I know you would never lay a
hand on me without a preacher sealing it. You
are too much a good man. Although if a
marriage was near, I might not be too much
against it."

"I very much doubt that, Addie. You are a
true lady."

"But not a lady you want to marry, I
guess. I just don't see what the matter is. I
know we've never had a normal courtship like
other people. I had it with Ashe, but you never
did. No box suppers down at the church, and
no picnics down by the Tuckasegee. If I was
younger, we would be meeting at corn
husking, candy pulls, and all sorts of things so
we could see each other. I consider our going
to church together and planting the garden
kind of like a courtship."

Addie placed a hand on my arm. "I do
love you. Can you just try to love me too? If
you want, we can sell this place and move to
Tennessee. It probably would not bring too
much money. Or we could keep the place and

give it to Davie when he is old enough to take a wife. That is, if he wanted to come back to the mountains."

She let go of my arm and turned to look out into the darkness. "I always felt this had to be God's garden place. I love it and know the good Lord made it beautiful with its rainbow of colors that change from season to season. I love the fog as it raises from the river and moves into the mountains about daybreak. It makes me feel like a cocoon, all snug and safe." She turned back to face me. "But I love you more. I can be packed as soon as you want to leave. Or we could stay till the last of the food is stored away for the winter and take it with us."

"I guess I do owe you an explanation. It's not you. It's yore name."

Addie? Fisher?"

"You're not who I thought you were. You're a Hooper."

"Yes, that's my birth name. But I would gladly take on Millsaps. I am certain that Davie would like to take your name too."

"I am not really a Millsaps. I am a Watson."

"But you told me you were Nathe Millsaps?"

"I lived with a cousin in Tennessee. Jemena Millsaps."

Addie didn't seem as upset about me being a Watson as I was about her being a

Hooper. "But why would you want to take her name? Did your Mama and Papa die?"

"Your Papa killed my Papa."

She jumped back like I had struck her. "You wuz Tucker Watson's boy?" Her eyes clouded with tears.

"I AM Tucker Watson's boy. Your family murdered mine."

She pushed her lips together real tight, like she was trying to keep from talking. It didn't work, if that was her plan.

"Do you know what Tucker Watson and his two brothers did to my Grandpa Amos Hooper and my uncle, Amos Junior? The Watson's planned a hunting trip and slipped and asked Amos junior to go with them. They knew nobody ever took him, and he wanted to hunt like the others. He was thirteen years old. He was born crippled in his feet. He couldn't keep up. The Watson's took him and left him in the woods. He was killed by a bear. My Papa and Grandpa Amos found him the next day. Grandpa Amos died when they found his body. He grabbed his chest and fell over the remains of Amos Junior's body. That's what they did. They knew he was crippled. They shouldn't oughta have taken him. It was pure meanness."

She breathed deep, and put her hand back on my arm. "That was them. This is us. I ain't killed nobody, and neither have you." She moved around to get in front of me and made me look at her. "Well, you haven't, have you?"

"No, not yet. But that was my family, and nobody did a thing about it. So I will."

"Nobody did a thing about Amos Hooper either, so maybe you and I just better get guns and have it right here. You want to kill me? Well, do you?"

"No, you didn't kill nobody. But you are wrong. I reckon they did do something about Amos and his son. They killed my family. Somebody has to pay. Don't you see?"

"Then let me pay for it. One that killed is dead. My papa didn't kill nobody. I heard him tell Mama it was Levi and Silas that did the killing, and Silas is dead and Levi is purt near. Let's just let it be over."

"They knocked my mama down and did horrible things to my family. Mama sent me to get help. While I was gone, they killed my Papa and two of my uncles. They kicked my cousin, Tercy, so baldy she died two days later. My sister was raped and never spoke another word until the day she just walked into the woods and was never seen again. Mama was blind from where they slung her against a nail that tore her eye."

"Stop it. I don't want to hear about it." She covered her ears with her hands.

I reached and pulled her hands down. "Addie, you have Hooper blood flowing through you. Hooper blood! You are not who I thought you was."

"It's just blood. Just red blood. There ain't no such thing as Hooper blood or Watson blood or Fisher blood. It's just red blood." She took her nails and scratched her wrist until the blood ran. "Just RED blood. There ain't no such thing as bad blood. See my blood. It looks just like yours."

I wouldn't look at her wrist again, although she kept poking it in my face.

"There is such a thing as bad blood to me. I watched Watson blood run out on the ground. Now I want to see Hooper blood run."

"Please don't do nothing to nobody. We can change things. We can bring this horrible feud to an end."

"I'll end it, but not like you want it done. My papa will not rest until I take revenge on the Hoopers for the killing. We have to have the last say. Don't you understand?

"You are not the man I thought you were. I thought you were a kind man that cared for me and my children. How does my name make any difference? I am still Addie."

"What I am going to do has to be done. I may live or I may die, but either way, I guess this is good-bye."

"Then just kill me and be over with it. If mine is Hooper blood, and it is Hooper blood you have to shed, then just take that gun of yores and shoot me. Maybe then you'll be happy. Go ahead and do it. Do it, I say. Take Davie to Mama and Papa. But kill me."

I took the gun up and aimed it at her. She stared into my eyes.

She turned and walked toward the house. She broke into a run about halfway there. I watched her leave like a man who sees the beauty of fall in the mountains when he knows for him there will be no spring.

I jerked the gun down. I took my pack, and ran. I spent the night down by the river, the place I had lived when I first came back to Jackson County.

Chapter 22

The moon was full, and it was like walking in the daylight all the way to the river. I laid down by the water and pushed my pack under my head. I was not sleepy. My mind wanted to think about Addie, but I wanted to consider Clay and the night I listened to them. They talked about going to church. You would think they were not the church-going type, murderers and all.

I imagined what it might have been like if they tried to join the church. Everybody in the area knew they did it. But with no witnesses like me or Mama to tell the real story, they could vouch for each other's whereabouts, even if it wasn't true. If there were two or three witnesses for them, there was no way you could prove a thing. Even if they were his brothers or other family.

Clay didn't seem like the man that had been in my house all those years ago, like he was changed. Maybe there had been a cold winter's night, and perhaps his mind got still enough that his conscience talked with him. I bet he didn't recount it to no preacher though…but maybe to his maker. Such a man would mend his ways, and he would either join a church or, if he had been a trunk member, he would start actively going to the house of God. Trunk members were those that had joined the church, but their papers lay in the trunk and they never darkened the door to the house of God.

That might be what had happened. But his seed had learned the way of their father and was ready to take up where he left off. Of course not Addie, but maybe Marshall would. Even if I stayed and did nothing, who's to say he wouldn't come after me one day. That is why I had to kill him. That and to do it for my Papa and his brothers. It was my duty. The Watson honor was at stake.

xxx

Next morning I left the river early and went to the store at East LaPorte. I had not been back there since I had bought seeds for Addie. There were men sitting on the front porch of the store swapping stories and shooting the breeze about weather and crops. Everyone stopped and looked at me.

"Howdy, don't let me hinder your visiting."

"We have us a stranger here, men." I looked from face to face at their laughter. "What's yer name?"

"Nathe."

"Nathe. Is that short for Nathan?"

I looked head on at the man that asked me. "Yes sir, it is."

"What's your family name?"

"Milsaps. My name is Nathe Milsaps."

"What brings you to these mountains? You some kind of law?"

"Naw."

"Maybe a peddler from up at Asheville?"

"Naw to that neither. I am from Tennessee."

"Tennessee, huh? What brings you here? Are you on the run from the law? Is that it, is the law looking for you?"

"Not that I know of."

They laughed, and my shoulders eased. It was then that I realized how much fear they put in me.

"He's that young man living up at Widow Fisher's house.. I saw him down here one day last spring. He was buying seeds and plants for a garden." Eyes stared at me as they waited for me to admit it. I didn't feel like I had been asked a question, so I kept quiet.

Another man spoke up. "You'd think she'd take up with one of the men from around here, if she was looking again. What would make a woman choose a Tennessee boy over a good mountain man? It just don't seem right." They laughed harder.

"Are you in line for the job?" Everyone laughed when the older man of the group asked it. "If so, I can send someone up to tell my daughter about it. Then I will shoot you, my son-in-law, and be done with it. We'll just say that some stranger from Tennessee saw you moving in on his territory and shot you down. Right boys?" They nodded.

"Aw, you know I was just a lollygagging him. I was speaking in general. True mountain women don't want boys like him. I am plenty happy with your daughter."

I used the time they argued with each other to move away. They commenced talking again about the weather and crops when I entered the open door of the store. I gathered ammunition and some jerky, supplies for the trip when I left. I had purposely saved skins for trading after I had foolishly used the last of my money on Addie's house. The men didn't notice when I stepped outside and moved to the side of the store out of their sight. I listened to their bickering and jokes.

Another man had come up in a wagon and stood in front of them.

"I hear tell your woman is having another youngun, Marshall."

My hands shook. *So was this Marshall Hooper*? It didn't take as long as I feared.

Another man piped up. "Heard your pappy, Clay, is back from Asheville."

The storekeeper came out and leaned against the post on the corner. He noticed me standing out of the sight of the others.

"It's true, Polly and I are expecting a baby by Christmas. And my Papa is back. They are up at my sister's house, I suppose." His voiced sounded almost exactly like his Papa's.

The storekeeper looked at me, realizing that I worked for Addie. I was glad he didn't say anything. Would the others? They had just mentioned that I worked for her. I felt like something was in my throat about the size of a tater.

I recognized Marshall's face from my first day at the store. If I had only known. It probably wouldn't have changed the outcome, but I had been so close to him. In my mind, I always thought I would know any one of them as soon as I saw them or heard their voice. He seemed like any other man, but deep inside of him was all the venom of a poisonous snake. All Hoopers are the same.

Jemena always said you cannot judge a man by the outside. Of course she was meaning that a man might look bad but still be good, but today I saw it differently. Did those other men know that the Hooper family were murderers?

I stared at the back of his head. I thought about all the things that I might do to him. Perhaps I would shoot him through and through. Then I could take his body that night and hang it from a tree in his front yard. Or maybe hang it in Clays' front yard. I could see his boots dangling at the end of his legs as they swang in the wind. I felt pleasure at the thought. My mind could see his Papa and Mama crying and moaning over the casket like my Mama had. Then Addie would walk up to the casket…

Marshall said, "Can I get about three yards of that cotton material you have? My wife has got to make some blankets for the baby."

One of the men yelled at Marshall as he walked into the store. "There was a man here earlier that works for your sister. Did you know she had a man living up there?"

I ran as fast as I could toward the river.

xxx

I tugged off my pants and shirt and washed them in the Tuckasegee. Washing without soap wouldn't get the stink out but maybe enough that I could hide downwind from Marshall, and he wouldn't smell me before I did what I had to do. The wind blew the bushes where the clothes hung.

The water was cold. Even in the hottest of weather, the Tuckaseege could be counted on to cool a body off. I dove in and swam underwater and came up further downstream than I thought I would. There stood Amps on the shore.

"Taking a bath, boy? It ain't even Saturday night." He laughed.

In all the time I had known him, I had never heard him laugh.

"Even a skunk needs a bath once in a while." I stood up and waded along the edge of the water back to where I had left my clothes.

"That they do. Even though they don't usually get them. I see you have washed your clothes too. I thought that widow woman did yer washing."

"She does, but I am moving on soon. I don't want to bother her with washing right now."

"Moving on, huh? So that decision you were fretting about. Have you made your choice? Did you get out of your system what you came to do?"

"I think I got a lot of wanderlust out. Yes."

"Wanderlust had nothing to do with it. I know it. You know it. There was lust, but it was for a heavier cause than you are letting on."

"Why don't you just leave me alone? You are always trying to find some kind of meaning for me being here. You are a nosy old fool."

"I may be nosy, and for sure, in my life I've been a fool. I've been trying to keep you from being the same. There is a lot about me you don't know. And I know more about you than I let on or that I can tell you."

"You don't know nothing about me. We are strangers, and I want to keep it that way. I thought you were my friend for a while, but you're not a friend."

"What? You think a friend just sits back and lets you make a fool of yourself without warning you? A friend wouldn't do that. Does a friend sit back and let you get yourself killed? Or kill someone and ruin your life?"

"I am not going to make a fool of myself. The thing that I need to do is an honorable thing, and you know nothing about it. To not take care of the matter would make me the fool."

"Honor is a good thing, when you can do it and stay honorable. When you can walk away with clean hands and a conscience without regret. I am going to say it. Revenge is like drinking salt water and expecting it to quench your thirst. It'll never do it. When you force that heavy boulder out into the open, it is going to roll back over you. It will take away everything that would make your life good. It will destroy you. You think it will make you happy, but you will be a walking corpse for whatever time you have left with breath in your body."

Revenge. How did he know? "You stay out of my business. I don't know who you are, but you've got to get away from me, or I'll kill you."

"Not likely, son…not likely. Suffering takes many forms. To watch someone you love as they die is a fate worse than death to many."

Exactly what I was thinking. And hoping.

"I watched my wife die at the hands of someone else. I hated that man. The taste of revenge was in my mouth. It felt impossible to stop myself, and I took care of them that murdered her. I ate, drank, and slept revenge until I did it."

I wish I had known this from the beginning. He could have helped me know what to do. "You did? How did you do it?"

"It don't matter how. But I now realize you cannot murder everyone that wrongs you. No matter how bad that wrong. Some acts *are* worthy of death, but to be their executioner only soils your soul, and makes you no better than them. I remember that sweet taste of revenge soured in my mouth and stomach. I thought it would have lasted, but it was bitter afterwards. It ate at my innards. The devil rode on the back of my horse every night I rode. He whispered in my ear how he had made a fool of me. I am a fool. I hope you won't be one."

My breeches were dry, and I slipped them on. When I looked back, Amps was gone.

Chapter 23

The sun sent light over Rich Mountain but had not yet risen. The churning of excitement and a slight sense of dread made goose flesh on my arms. Today was the day that I would put one Hooper in the hole, maybe two, just like they had Papa, his brothers, and Tercy.

The early morning shadows were fading into bright daylight as I left the road and cut across Rich Mountain to Horney Head Mountain. This trail was the only route from Marshall's house to the mill.

My search showed the best place to lay in wait was in a laurel thicket. I had found it in the bend of the road. It was where one fork led to the mill, and the other rounded the mountain and headed off in the direction of Cullowhee. It was right below Buck Creek falls. The laurel was thick as Amp's eyebrows. Two times I had to stop and sharpen the blade on the hatchet. I would hack limbs back and pull them out to the back of the thicket. The room I made was square, about eight feet in either direction. The road side was dense with bushes of laurel. There were only a few leaves to cut off to create an opening large enough to peek out and stick the barrel of the gun through. I also made a path out the back. I cleared it to about a quarter mile below the ambush site to where a bear path ran down the mountain side antigoglin and led to the Tuckasegee. Another mile and a half down the mountain. This path would then come back out on the road. If someone on the trail found the body, they would never see me.

I walked a half mile up the mountain and retraced my steps back down. The trip allowed me to see what Marshall would see as he came to my hiding place. There was a thin section just before he got to me that might let him set an eye on me. I took some of the cut laurel vines and piled it thick to fill the hole. This made a better wall to hide behind. It should not wilt for several days with the cool days and nights. It would look like natural growth.

xxx

One full day had passed since I scouted out the ambush place. I had no idea what time Marshall would start his trip down the mountain to the mill. Spending the night in the woods was the best assurance to be in place when he came by. The night was cold on the mountain, and the trees were in the midst of the change of fall. Rich colors were scattered like flowers on Decoration Day at the cemetery. I pulled some of the vine back into the area I cleared, and made them a protection from the cold ground. Inside the pack were the clothes that Addie had given me as well as the ones I brought from Tennessee. It had not seemed right to take the ones Addie gave me, but I was sure glad I had. I spread them on the laurel leaves and laid down.

Darkness fell quick, and it was impossible to see my hand before my face. Nothing left to do but sleep, but it was a fitful slumber, to say the least, with dreams troubling me. Mama was with me. I was a tiny lad sitting on her knee, and she was singing to me. I took my hand and felt of her hair. Mama put me down and stood. She walked a little ways and turned back to look at me. She smiled at someone over my shoulder, and I turned and there was Papa. He looked the same. I looked at my hands, and they were now big. I had become a grown man in my dream. It was winter

because the leaves were off the trees. The trees
were gray, and the limbs were knocking
against each other in the wind. There was a
blue-gray fog settling on us, and suddenly I
couldn't see Mama anymore. Papa spoke, and
I turned back to him to see what he had said. A
hand came around from behind Papa's head
and grabbed him. A knife cut deep into his
neck. Blood shot into my face, and I fought at
it with both hands. I screamed.

At least I thought I screamed. I don't
know if I did or not. I opened my eyes and
water hit me on the jaw. Fog or light rain had
covered the leaves and dripped into my face.

The morning was cool, and the clouds and
fog in the small room felt like a coat, clinging
in just the right places. The thicker it gathered,
the safer I felt. If it hung low until Marshall
came, that was all the better. One look out the
peep hole assured me I could see him good
enough for a fatal shot, but not until he was
very close. I loaded my gun and found a space
where I could see down the path to my left for
a ways. When he was in sight, I would still
have time to aim and then shoot when it was
certain I would not miss. Right in front of my
peep hole.

Almost all my life had been waiting and
planning for this day. The unknown target now
had a name. Marshall Hooper. My heart
pounded. It would be so easy to kill him. All I
had to remember was how Clay, his Papa, had
hit my Papa with the butt of his gun until he

screamed with pain. Marshall was only fifteen at that time. He would be twenty-six, almost twenty-seven now. It didn't matter that he had not seen his Papa and the others do it. What I really wanted to do was to take his head off and tie it to the seat of that wagon and send it back up to his house. Or maybe to Clay's house.

It would be several hours before he passed so I lay back down on the ground and waited. Limbs crunched and I grabbed my gun.

"It's just me…Amps. Sorry I scared you boy. What you doing here?"

"I…I…. Amps it's none of your business. What are *you* doing here?"

"I think I may know your plans. You have talked a lot about feuds with me over this summer. Could it be that you have aught with someone and plan on taking care of it today?"

Amps hoiked and spit. He looked at my bed from the night before. His eyes moved over the hiding place I had made for myself. He rubbed his mouth and wiped it on his britches.

He looked me in the eye and spoke slowly. "A person would almost think that the dirt in these mountains would be red. Not this black, rich dirt." He stooped and grabbed a fist full of dirt and let it sift through his fingers back to the ground. "Feuds have been long and have soaked the soil in the blood. Lives that were meant to be lived long and enjoyed by family were taken out in a fit of anger. There

are days I wish I had never left my homeland.
But I have told you that before. I wander
around looking at the sites that men have died
and wonder what would have happened if we
had just talked first instead of killing. I don't
rightly think it would have worked every time,
but maybe sometimes. What is it about a man
that thinks he is always right or that he has to
be right? What convinces him that what one
does to you has to be done back to make things
fair? Where did we learn that life would be, or
ever could be, fair."

I didn't know if he wanted me to answer
or not, so I waited. He turned and looked at
me. I turned away from him and pretended to
clean beggar lice from my shirt.

"Usually a man that kills to settle a matter
feels he must inflict great injury or death on
his enemy but have less loss to himself. He
just does not reflect long enough to see the ill
he brings to his own children. His family. I
always knew that I taught my family to farm
by working with them right alongside me.
Why does a man not see that everything he
does is teaching?"

His words were rough and scratchy. "Do
you really want to teach your children the way
of feuding?"

"I don't have no children."

"You think it's going to end here? It
won't you know. Someday or sometime, they
will find out who did it, and then you or
someone dear to you will die. Mountain people

have learned to be patient, if nothing else. It may not be tomorrow or next week or even next month, but it comes around again. If you want to honor your family name, whatever that family name truly is, then keep your children safe. For you to kill another man will threaten their lives. You never know from what laurel thicket will come the shot that breaks a mother's heart. Or your heart. Some mama or papa will answer the knock at the door, and someone will tell them that their son or her husband is dead. In a matter of time, some father will find his daughter or a brother will find his sister raped and murdered."

Did he know about Tercy? Why did he know so much about this?

"Exactly who is the person you plan on killing today, Nathe?"

My hand shook as I placed the gun on the ground beside me. "You just need to get out of here, Amps. I don't want you here. It's best you don't see this or have any recollection of it. Get on back down to where you live. It has nothing to do with you."

"I may not know anything about this killing, but I can recollect seeing more dead bodies in my lifetime than I care to think about. It's a fact that revenge is only carried out when it's been nursed by someone with a lot of pain. You think it will ease that pain. But it won't boy. Take it from me, it surely won't. The pain will be just as great and the emptiness still there.

"We don't have much way of getting any law in here. Never have. And because they don't come, we make our own laws and try to make people live by them as best we know how. It can only be expected that one or two will decide they are beyond the arms of the law and live and die to themselves, and make others do the same. In the past, we did what we needed to do to survive. Make a living and protecting what was ours. The ruckus came when someone disagreed on that very thing. They thought it was theirs and I thought it was mine. The only real way to settle it was for one of us to die. No one thought about talking it out or coming to an agreement."

I leaned my head to the side and acted like I was scratching my face with my shoulder. It was easier to wipe the tears that way without Amps seeing them.

"If a man picks at a sore, it festers and bleeds. It would be best to leave it be and let it heal. Nathe, one part of you is broken and the other is bitter. Your heart is set on fire. You have a decision. Put out that fire or get even. You think if you fan that fire of hatred it will make it easy to take a man's life. But the hand that sets the fire gets caught up the flames. You get snared in the trap you set. Set this man and his boy free, Nathe."

"Don't you see? This was not done just one time. I need to kill the seed that carries the hatred of the Watsons." He knew everything. I don't know how, but he knew. Right down to who it was.

"You have made your own prison out of the hate. You guard it like a stockade and are more caged by it than those you hate."

"Just go away! Leave me be."

"You think I don't know what it feels like to lay in bed at night an feel like you are the only one to take care of things. Maybe we were taught wrong. Perhaps the stopping of bloodshed is for just one man to turn the other cheek. You are that one man."

That was exactly like I felt, as if it was up to me to get it done. If there was any cheek turning it had to be by someone else. "Amps you need to get out of here."

"Do you think this churning you have felt for ten years will be satisfied when you get your revenge?"

He knew more than just who I wanted to kill? Ten years? Who told him? *Stop it. Stop it* I screamed it in my mind.

Amp's looked tired and weak. "I would to God that all the graves in Poverty Hill Cemetery and every other graveyard were only those that die of disease or old age. The grave is cruel enough without going there with the weight of a body hanging to your soul. Which is what happens if you commit murder. Or even have the feeling for the need of a murder. In this life you become a vagabond trying to run from the guilt, and eternity won't give you peace. Guilt is not a feeling. It's a person that talks in your ear day and night. He reminds you of everything you've done, and what you might have done differently. But it's too late to do anything about it after you die."

I stopped him.   "You think it's murder to give someone an equal payback for their actions? A tooth for a tooth? You seem bent on judging me without knowing everything that happened. This revenge is right and reasonable! It's my family duty. It's not murder. It's justice."

"I promise you I know more than you realize. You need to listen to reason, boy."

I put both hands on the sides of my head and pushed hard against my ears. "Please, just stop, Amps. Leave me be. You think you know about this, but you don't. You don't know me at all. If you did, you would stay away. I can't stop what I am doing now. The final payback is here. It was why I was spared, to make sure that I could avenge the murders of my family. To get even."

"Revenge may make you even with them. They in turn need to get even in their sight. Letting it pass would make you better. May God be with you, son."

I felt sick and stuck my head between my knees. My hands squeezed over my ears to shut out his words.

xxx

The wagon wheels rattled, and I jumped up and ran to the peep hole and looked out. Chains clattered as the wagon came nearer. I wondered if Amps would spoil it and looked back to see what he was doing. He was nowhere to be seen.

The boy was talking to his dad, and I could hear their laughter. It reminded me of my Papa and me on a trip to the mill. It was one of the happiest memories I had…when it was just me and Papa. The perfect time to cut him down. I rocked back and forth making sure I did not get too hasty and spoil it by my impatience. *Just wait till they are just past the curve and directly in front of me. Be patient.* I trembled with excitement. Or was it fear. I felt sick to my stomach again. *I have not eaten…that is why. Revenge is mine…today…right now. Blood for blood. The future is nothing until I can pay just dues for the past.*

The horses passed. The wagon was beside me. I put the rifle to my shoulder and eyed the bead at the end waiting for it to line up with Marshall's head. My trigger finger shook. I willed my mind to see the blood the way it looked on Tercy's dress after she puked. I thought about the fear in Mama's eyes. I looked around the room in my mind and saw the Watsons as they lay in heaps and moaning with pain. My finger steadied.

The horse reared, and Marshall grabbed at his son with his right arm before he fell from

the wagon. The rifle slipped from my
shoulder, and I lost sight of the bead as I
watched them.

Marshall grabbed his gun with his left
hand. He stood and raised the gun. His
standing body was the perfect target. It was
like it was meant to be. I pulled the gun back
to my shoulder and aimed. Kill him and let his
son watch him die. He couldn't see me, and I
could escape out the back of the laurel thicket,
no one knowing I had done it. Sliding across
the road had been the biggest rattler I have
ever seen and it had spooked the horses. It had
set Marshall up like a deer in my sights.

The sound of the gunshot bounced from
tree to tree through the valley and could be
heard for miles.

Chapter 24

Amps was nowhere to be seen in the laurel thicket. Probably, he had left before the gunshot. I grabbed my pack and ran through the path I had made. Near a mile through the woods, I came to the road that comes off Horny Head Mountain. The road was muddy from a rain shower, and I walked in the ruts of a wagon. Half way down, I left the road and followed Pistol Creek. Panther Hollow was where I could cut back and follow the lower ridge out. I stopped before I left the creek and laid down on my stomach and drank.

"I heard the gunshot. So, did you kill my boy?" I tripped over my own feet as I tried to get up and caught myself on my hands.

"Clay. You sure can slip up on a man."

"I asked you a question." Clay's face was white, and he looked old and tired. He was breathing hard and holding his chest.

I turned and faced him. "What makes you think that I meant to kill Marshall?"

"Addie came to my house early this morning. She had been traveling since before sun-up to get to me. It took her a couple of days of thinking about a conversation you and her had to bring her to the conclusion you were out to murder her brother. She was afraid. She was crying so hard. She said you were really a Watson, and she was pretty sure you were going to murder Marshall. Is it true? Did you kill my boy? I heard the gunshot." Clay sat down on a tree trunk and continued to hold his chest.

Are you feeling poorly? Why are you holding your chest?"

"I came as fast as I could to stop you. It looks like it is too late." He searched my face. If he was looking for remorse, he would not see any. "Today is his birthday. My only living son. Addie's older brother by one year. How could you do it?"

"How could I do it? How could you and Levi and Silas and Pierce do what you did? You took my family."

"So you are that little boy in the cabin that day. I wondered what happened to you. I looked for you, but nobody seemed to know where you went. Some thought you were dead. That you went crazy like that sister of yours did, and just went off in the woods and died."

"So you looked for me even a year later. After Rachel died? What were you going to do? Kill me? Surely you knew you had gotten away with it by then."

"I wasn't looking for you in order to kill you. I just wanted to know you were alive."

"Sure you did. You wanted to make sure I wouldn't talk. That's all you wanted. You would have me believe that you wanted to make sure I was alright?"

"It was years and years ago that this happened. Even a year later, I was a different person."

"No, you are still Clay Hooper, a man that killed my family and had no mercy."

"It's true I was there and am as guilty as the next. I've done many a grievous wrong. I've asked my maker to forgive me, and I'm asking you to forgive me, too. It was a mean thing we did. My brothers and I were hot tempered and out for our set of revenge with your family. It don't make it right, but that's just how it was. It's a wonder that this land can grow a thing, it is so filled with the blood." He sounded like Amps.

His face blurred through my tears. "My Mama saw my Papa killed. If I had not run, you all would have killed me too. And you say this thing was a mean thing to do. Mean does not justly describe what you did."

He took a deep breath and raked his hands at his tears, his lower lip shook. He shoulders drooped. If he was looking for sympathy, I had none. "Now my son is dead too. There's no one left but me and you. Just shoot me too. I druther be dead myself than go home and tell his mama and Addie that he's dead. What did you do with the boy? Or did you find a way to kill him too? Can't have shot him. There was only one gunshot. Are you going to wait until he's grown? Let him live a little while without a papa like you did? Is that your plan?"

"I think that would be justice."

His eyes were like fire and cut into mine. They never left my face, and he continued to hold his chest. His face screwed up with pain. "I am trying to find what my Addie could have seen in you to think that you was worthy of her love. It's just not there. Did you purposely find her and let her love you just to hurt her?"

"It never entered my head that she could be a Hooper."

"That boy of hers thinks you hung the moon. You hauled out a lot of hurt from this. It must make you deeply satisfied."

"I did not want to hurt Addie. She is the finest woman I know. I could not have loved Davie or Clare any more had they been mine."

"If you really loved her, you couldn't have done this killing. Only a man with heart of iron could do it." He slid back on the log and leaned his head against the trunk of the tree. "I thought this was all over with years ago. I've lived longer than I deserved for my sins." He laid his gun to the side. "Go ahead and get it over with. Kill me, and be on your way. Talking does no good at a time like this."

I didn't answer. He stood and stretched his arms outward and screamed. "Just shoot me. Get it over with. Shoot me, I beg you. Do it now."

There was laughter in the distance and the familiar rattle of trace chains. Horse hooves pounded on the ground. Loose boards on the wagon slapped on the wagon frame as the wooden wheels hit the ruts. The voices were obviously Marshall and Glee.

Clay stared at me in disbelief. "You let them live? You made me think they were dead."

"I let you believe what you wanted to believe."

He fought to raise his body upright. His hand shook as he reached down for his hat. He leaned forward too much and staggered. I reached out and grabbed his arm to steady him.

His shoulders shook, and tears rolled down his weathered face, running into the wrinkles that started on each side of his nose making a crevice that let the tears slide into his mouth. "My son. My grandson. Mercy was given to me. Thank you, Nathe."

"Grandpa." Glee stood and shouted, pointing his finger toward us.

"What you doing up here, Pa?" Marshall looked from me to his papa and saw the tears. "Is everything ok?"

"Everything is just fine boy. Had to come and tell my son how happy I am he was born. Happy birthday, son."

Still not totally satisfied, he asked, "You know this man?"

"Well yes I do. He's the man that has been helping Addie over at her place all spring and summer."

Marshall tied the reins to the front of the wagon and got down. "You never told me that."

"I'm sure glad to see you son." Clay slapped Marshall on the back.

"He saved our lives back there. We were coming along the road just minding our own business, and there was a rattler that was quiled up, then stretched itself out and looked as long as a sapling tree. It came right toward Ned, and he reared up raising that wagon clean off the ground. It knocked Glee out of his seat and to the ground right near that snake. I jumped off and rolled away. That rattler was moving right toward Glee. Right out of the blue I heard a gunshot. Knocked that rattler into a spinning fit. Don't think he killed him but sure put him in a turmoil. He raced into the woods. I jumped up and grabbed the reins of Ned who was pawing and rearing up, jerking that wagon forward and backward. This man picked up Glee and pulled him out from where the wagon was about to roll over him."

Glee pulled up his shirt and showed the scrape across his back and down his left arm. "Knocked the breath clean out of me, Grandpa. That rattler was taller than I am. He was just a dancing his rattlers back and twisting and a turning trying to get to me."

I went back to the log for my pack and gun.

"Papa, do you want to ride with us to the mill?"

"Sure. Give me a little spell with Nathe if you can wait."

"I can." Marshall went to the back of the wagon and checked on the load of corn.

Clay stuck out his hand. "I can't ever tell you how much I appreciate yore restraint. There's plenty of blame. Neither side has any bragging rights as to their destructive deeds."

My heart knew it was true. "When it came down to it, I couldn't kill him. My plan was to do it, but there were lots of voices in my head begging me not to. Addie's and Amps for starters. Mama and Davie."

"Amps?"

"Yeah. It's this old man that keeps showing up wherever I am. He acted like he knew every one of yall, but I'm not really sure who he is."

"It's strange but Amps was what we called…"

"Papa are you about ready to go. It's going to take all day going to the mill. I'm thinking I don't want to be coming home this way in the dark."

"I'm ready son." We walked to the wagon.

"I think I'll go back home to Addie. She will be happy it ended this way. If she came to you, she was probably scared I'd kill her brother. I don't think she would have made it this year without my help. I am thinking I will ask her to marry me."

Marshall slapped his knee. "A wedding. Now that would be a good thing for Addie. That son of hers needs a man to help around the house."

"We will see what she says. She might not be as anxious as you think she is to marry me. Not after the last few days we've had."

"All couples have their squabbles. She'll be forgiving, or I don't know my sister very well." He smiled and nodded toward me. "Giddap Ned." Glee was lying in the back of the wagon on top of the corn, and Clay was sitting by Marshall.

I could see me and Papa again in my mind, on our way to the mill talking and laughing. If I had taken Marshall's life, it would not have brought back Papa. Amps was right. It was past time to let the hate die.

Marshall stopped a little ways down the road to straighten the reins. They thought I was gone. But I heard Clay mutter, "Son, he's a Watson."

Maybe all the hate hadn't died in the heart of a certain Hooper.

The trip off the mountain didn't bring the peace I had hoped for. If it was not over with them, could it really be over for me? All I could do was go back to Addie and see what happened. I looked down the road, and there stood Amps. *Not again.* My toe stubbed on a rock, and I looked down to break my fall. When I looked up, Amps was gone. I guess he had no more wisdom to give. I felt a little disappointed.

CHAPTER 25

It was a moonless night, with thick dark clouds covering the light of the stars. But I was fixed on going to Addie. She had suffered all day wondering if her only living brother and her Papa were alive. I was pretty sure she didn't care a lick if I was living or not, but the thought of her having a broken heart pushed me to reassure her.

There was no fire down at Amps, and he was nowhere to be seen. It was probably the first time I had not seen a fire there in quite some time. Even in the heat of the summer, he had that fire burning. Cooking something, heating water, or standing staring into the flames or up on the mountain. I wished that I had made Clay finish what he was going to tell about him. He seemed to know who I was talking about. I would ask him about it the next time I saw him, if there was a next time.

It was asking a lot for Addie to forgive me. But if it was true that she loved me like I loved her, surely we could make a life together. All the dead people were just that…dead. Nothing we did or didn't do would bring them back. It wasn't being disloyal to them, for they couldn't feel or think or hear us. All those years of letting Papa fill my head with the need for revenge was all in my mind. I don't know what happens for sure when you die, just what the church says, but I didn't think a person would be overly concerned about the affairs of this life.

I felt pretty much like a man let out of a prison must feel. Free from the chains that I had carried. If a hundred pound sack of corn had dropped from my shoulders, I couldn't have felt any lighter than I did right now. Even knowing that Addie might not be forgiving, It was still a relief to know that revenge was past. It was like a poison that killed the person that drank it, even if he still was breathing.

The lamps were all blown out, and the house was dark. It would not be good to wake her or Davie. I sat down quietly on the steps and stared into the thick darkness. All my

hopes that she might forgive me were being
squeezed out like the star's light by the clouds.

"Why would you come back here, Nathe
Milsaps? Or Nathe Watson I should be calling
you." Her voice was dry and crackly like she
had the croup. She was sitting behind me on
the porch, and I could only feel her presence
but not see her.

"You scared me to death. I thought you
were asleep."

"Sleep? You think I can sleep knowing
my Papa and brother are both probably
somewhere dead in the woods? Did you cut off
their head and put them on pike poles, too? Is
that why you are back here? Are you going to
stick them in my yard so I can tell Davie how
the Watson family got revenge on us Hoopers?
Do I make him promise to find a Watson and
kill him too, so as to take this on to another
generation or two, or even three?"

"Addie…"

"If that is what you are planning to do,
then I will take care of killing a Watson
myself. Don't want my son to have to do it."
The gun cocked and I felt rather than saw her
pull it up and aim it at me.

"Addie…please listen for just a spell.
Your Papa is not dead and neither is
Marshall."

She started to bawl. She uncocked the gun
and laid it to her side. The next thing I knew,
she threw her arms around me from behind

and put her face in my neck. "They're not dead? You didn't kill them?"

"No, I couldn't do it?" I pulled her around to my lap and held her like a little baby and rocked her as she cried. "I am so sorry you worried, that I made you worry. I wanted to do it, but I couldn't. All I could think about was you and how you never did anything but good to me or anybody else. You didn't deserve that. All you ever did was love, and all I ever did was hate. But your love made my hate melt like a spring snow. I tried to keep hating and talking myself into killing them. I couldn't do it."

She didn't answer me, and I quit talking. We just sat like that in the dark. Me holding her tight and rocking back and forth and her face pushed against my chest.

xxx

The water felt good as I poured it over my back and chest. Clean. I felt like I had been dirty as when I had plowed all day and washed the grit and grime away. The guilt was gone. The voices inside my head were silent today, and nobody was pushing me to hunt down someone and kill him. It was like I had been reborn. My life was going to start over. The other days were like a dream of a little boy that was in pain all his life and now was at rest. Like he died and I was resurrected in his place and could finally live.

Addie's hand ran down my back and wiped at the water. "How are you feeling today?"

"I turned and took her in my arms and pulled her close.

"I feel like a new man. Happy for maybe the first time since I was a child." I set her to the side and finished bathing.

"Now don't you be too new a man. I liked the other one pretty good. At least part of him. The one that was a good Papa for my children and worked hard to make sure we had food and supplies for the winter."

"That part ain't changed. I still feel that I need to take care of you and Davie, that I want to be around here for a long time to come."

"Don't think I need no hired hand now. Maybe I can find you a better job. One that has a little better pay and some side benefits." She smiled a shy little smile and stepped closer to me. She stopped and looked me straight in the eye. "That is if you want that kind of arrangement. You might not be wanting the same thing as me."

"You think I don't? I do want the same thing. If you are agreeable, I will go down to the valley and find the preacher and see if he will come back up here and marry us."

"Do you love me, Nathe? I know that I am a few years older than you and have a ready-made family. Not what a young man usually wants, I don't guess. But I will do my dead level best to be a good wife and help you make a living and feed the family. I won't shirk any work. Nothing is too hard. And if it's in your mind to go back to Tennessee, I will pack our belongings and we will go there. I just want to be with you. That is if you feel the same."

She let out a squeal as I swung her up across my shoulder and took her to the porch and sat her in the swing. "I think this thing ought to be done right. Addie will you take me as your husband. I promise to love you and be the best husband I know how to be. We won't speak of this feud no more. It is gone and past. The dead are quiet in their graves, and we will be quiet here about it too while we are alive. Will you marry me?"

"What's going on out here? Mama, I thought you said Nathe was gone and never coming back. What is he doing here and down on one knee in front of you, and you just a screaming to beat Nancy?"

"You just hush now Davie, I got to answer a question that he has just asked me." She took my weathered face in her hands and leaned forward until her eyes were level with mine. "I will surely marry you, Nathe…What will our last name be?"

"I am Nathe Millsaps Watson. We are who we are." There was no reason to shirk from the name my Papa gave me. It was time to quit living a lie.

"I will marry you Nathe Watson. I love you and I want to be your wife until I die."

"Whoooop! Mama, are you really going to marry Nathe? Will he really be my Papa?"

"He's your Papa from this day on. Yours and Clare's that lays in the cold, cold ground down in the graveyard."

"And who knows, son, you may have a few brothers and sisters too." I ruffled his thick hair.

Davie danced around. "That pulley bone from the kitchen or that hot water on the steps…something worked. I knew Grandma would know what to do."

Addie and I laughed.

Tears flooded Addie's eyes, and she threw her arms around me. She planted a kiss on my cheek and covered it with her hand.

"I tell you what, Addie, you go and fix us some breakfast, and then I will get astride old Maude and go and get that preacher."

Chapter 26

I stopped by Aunt Linny's place on the way to find the preacher for marrying. I wanted her to know that I could tell people who I really was, and it was going to be fine.

Linny congratulated me and told me a story. "I had a dream last night and it was about you. In that dream, your Grandpappy, Cling Watson, we called him Amps, called out to me. I was walking by his place. It was cold as January on Rich Mountain and he was standing by a fire. "Amps been waiting on you" he said. He was about the age he was when he died. He had on a green checkered shirt. I would have thought he would have had on some clothing that I remembered him wearing but he didn't. There was snow on the ground, and he didn't even have on a coat, mind ye. Just standing there by a fire that burnt about half way between the house and that pole barn. He was looking up toward Rich Mountain, way up toward the top. He motioned me over by the fire and said to me. 'I want my grandson, Nathe, to have my piece of land as his own…this home place for him and his family. He has three boys and four girls, and he needs to be able to make a fair living for them.' I assured him I would take care of that."

My knees felt weak. I sat down in a chair. "You say you called him Amps?"

"Sure enough. Everyone just called him Amps. I got an old picture of him somewhere. An old tin one."

There was a buzzing in my head, and things starting getting dark. I leaned my head against the back of the chair. That went away, and I yelled for Aunt Linny.

"Keep your boots on. I found that there picture. Here it is."

I looked into the face that I had learned to know quite well the past year. It was Amps, just like I knew him.

"He died about a year before you was born. It was about this time of the year. He got caught out in the weather without a coat and took pneumonia and just up and died. That was why I was surprised that he knew anything about you. But it was a dream. Still I plan to do what he asked me to do. Your uncle Robert was the eldest, and we farmed the homeplace until Robert got killed. All the older children got places of their own and have no interest in it. But it does make sense that you have it as it joins Addie's place and that will be yours, too, when you marry."

"I appreciate it, Aunt Linny. It will help us a lot."

"Don't thank me. It's him you should be obliged to." She twisted her head and looked up.

"Aunt Linny, did he say 'Amps been waiting on you' a lot of times?"

"Shore he did. It became a family saying once we all knew the story."

"What was the story?"

"The story about the time he first said it, I reckon. Your Grandpa Amps was not what you would call a person of good and upright standing for a big portion of his life. The story of the feuding between Hoopers and Watsons is a known fact among these parts. Amps once killed a Hooper in his early years. Later on, he was hainted by that Hooper, he said. But more than that, the devil himself tormented Amps on many occasion. I once saw Amps come into our house, white as ghost. He said that the devil jumped behind him on his horse and rode all the way from the Tuckasegee River to the house. The horse was spooked by it too and ran as hard as it could all the way to the barn.

But Amps could never blow Lucifer off the back of that horse. He said the devil just kept saying "ye killed Cabe Hooper. I seen you do it, and you are mine." The first few times that happened Amps lay up in bed for days afterwards. One day Amps returned from selling furs at a place on Mt. Sterling. It got dark just as he got to the Tuckaseege. He said he just stopped on this side of the river and waited for the devil to get on and Amps said, "Amps been a-waiting on you." Never seemed as scared after that. After Amps passed on, sometimes we would say to each other, when we thought the other person has done, something bad 'Amps been waiting on you' like the devil was going to get you. It's just a saying."

"I had heard it before but never really knew why anyone said that."

"Don't you be worrin' about Amps. The preacher said that he made it right with his maker just before he died. Amps told his sons to not be feuding, but I guess the advice was a little late coming as he had taught them contrary. I heard the preacher say that 'they that live by the sword will die by the sword', and that has happened to this family for generations. You all lovey-dovey and marrying yourself to a Hooper woman is the final signing of peace I suppose. I hope anyways."

I reached into my pocket and pulled out the knife Amps had given me. "Did you ever see this before?"

"That looks like the knife that Amp's brothers got him from a trader on one of their supplies trips to Asheville. It was the Christmas after Amps killed Cabe Hooper in November. They told him it was to remind him of family honor. But Amps lost it about a year before he died, while we were at the cemetery when Uncle Rubin Watson was buried. Where did you find it?"

"Somebody gave it to me. They told me it would mean a lot to me someday. That maybe I could give it to my children.

"Thanks Aunt Linny for everything, but I need to be moving along."

xxx

On the way out, I stopped by Amp's place to see if I could see him. From the road, I waded through waist high grass trying to find the place where he had built a fire and we had sit and talked. There was no sign of a fire or anything that looked disturbed like someone had been there in years. The porch on the house where I had gotten water that first night was falling in and no place to set a bucket could be seen. Chills ran up my back, and my arm hairs stood up.

I know good and well that I talked to Amps on numerous occasions right here. Little things came back to my mind. Those times that I was walking and he just suddenly appeared with me and I never heard him coming, even though I am a skilled hunter and trapper. No noises ever got past me without my recognizing it. His knowledge of things that I was thinking or places I was going without me mentioning it. I had heard tell of haints and listened to a fair amount of ghost stories in my life but thought they were just that…stories. No truth to them. But there was just no explaining it away. Nearly a whole year of my life spent with a ghost. But without him, I probably would be dead today. I was determined to finish off the last of those Hoopers, and more likely than not would have gotten myself killed in the process. All those times he told me that feuding was not the way. He was speaking from experience.

What about all those children he mentioned? Addie only had a boy and a girl. And Clare passed. Did that mean I would have three more girls and two sons of my own? Someone to carry on the Watson name?

The End

1: To Miss Lizzie Chester Hood, "Wanted a Hand To Hold My Own", Sept. 8, 1855. By Bernard Covert.

2: Welsh Lullaby written in the 1800's.

CPSIA information can be obtained at www.ICGtesting.com
Printed in the USA
LVOW131332090912

298028LV00001B/4/P